MW00763401

The Secret First Lady

ROSE BUSH

AuthorHouse™
1663 Liberty Drive
Bloomington, IN 47403
www.authorhouse.com
Phone: 1-800-839-8640

First published by AuthorHouse 4/27/2011

ISBN: 978-1-4567-5053-4 (sc)
ISBN: 978-1-4567-5055-8 (dj)
ISBN: 978-1-4567-5054-1 (ebk)

Library of Congress Control Number: 2011904818

Printed in the United States of America

Photographer (Author's Photo): Arthur Usherson
Cover Design: Charles C.J. Mack

I would like to thank God, who should always be the head of my life and even when I fall short he still blesses me and protects me.

This book is dedicated:

To my mother, who loves me in spite of me and has never let me down.

To my uncle David; thanks for believing in me and always encouraging me.

Raylynn and Rya, the most beautiful people in my life; you two bring me so much joy and motivation.

To my Grandma, my aunts, and siblings, you all have played a very unique role in my life.

To all of my friends, who believed in me on the days that I didn't even believe in myself.

To the people who have let me down, I thank you for helping me to build a great character.

Last but certainly not least I want to thank ME.

I thank you all from the bottom of my heart for encouraging me to not only dream, but to also follow through.

I love you all.

Prologue

It's almost comical all the places life will take you before you realize your purpose for living, if you ever truly recognize what that purpose may be. After all the pain, stress, and mental anguish, only then can one truly appreciate tranquility. Sometimes it takes for one to move outside of their comfort zone just to become motivated; or to recognize their self-worth and love the person that God designed them to be. After moving to metro Atlanta, Rachel Jones realized there was life after what felt like a spiritual death. Why not tell her story? The good, bad, and the ugly that made her the exceptional woman she came to be. What's important is how we handle the truth. What a liberating experience it is to overcome the barriers that seemed impossible to conquer. Rachel Jones is more than a conqueror . . . and so are you.

Table of Contents

Chapter One

Temporary Insanity

Love; that four letter word can turn even the classiest chick insane. A Harvard education or a fat bank account can't even withstand the spell that love puts on you; material things cannot replace emotional necessities—well at least not in genuine situations. Rachel Jones was considered a five-star chick and had accomplished many things in her short-lived era. Although she was now a single mother of two, she had it going on mentally, physically, and financially. She was living a life that women twice her age only read about or imagined. She was an educated executive woman, who didn't boast about material things.

Her chocolate physique was well toned and it was obvious she worked out on a regular basis. Her smile could melt even the hardest ruffian. Her hair was so beautiful, bouncing with every step she took. Ms. Jones was fancy; however her favorite stores were Banana Republic and Bebe. She was so this and that to everyone one living outside of her world looking in, yet no one truly understood her struggle or the reason behind her hustle. She defined the saying, "from nothing to something." This Nia Long look-a-like had done it all and had it all done to her;

still she refused to fall victim to her circumstance. By the time she had reached the age of 25, her second child was 3 and Curtis, the father of her children, and ex-husband was showing no love or support. They had gotten married fresh out of high school, against her parents' wishes; never did she expect for it to end in divorce.

Having just finished her MBA, she decided she would show him that neither her nor their children needed him to survive. Besides they were total opposites. She worked her butt off, while Curtis slung crack-cocaine in the streets and chain-smoked marijuana. Knowing they weren't meant to be, she continued to hold on for their children's sake. She felt that children needed both parents; in fact she believed her life would have been a lot less fortunate in a single parent home. Financially life was great, but something was lacking.

Rachel drove down Walt Stephens Road as she recaptured her past life events prior to moving to Georgia. *I still can't believe I had to go through all of that, just to get here.* Rachel thought about Curtis periodically and their life in Ohio. She wondered if they could ever be the dynamic duo again, but those thoughts would quickly be interrupted by painful memories and then she would laugh.

Rachel loved her children, nevertheless, she was often away from them promoting her business and developing more ways to create more revenue. She independently built an investment banking firm on a small loan and a big dream. She continued to drive as she thought about the final breaking point of their marriage. She had to depart from Ohio and go to China for 6 months. Her business trips were generally no more than a month here and there, but for a multi-million dollar deal, who wouldn't take a six month hiatus? She remembered the day as if it just happened. After packing her bags and saying goodbye to her family, she gave her husband an ultimatum. "Curtis, when I come back, I better not hear any talk about you being in the streets. I want you out of the game. Babe, you can be my business partner. You seem to forget you are married to a millionaire."

It wasn't that Curtis was envious of his wife; well maybe a little, but as a man he'd rather take his chances on the streets before he saw himself working for his wife. Rachel had her own empire and he wanted something he could call his own. Curtis was in and out of foster homes when he and Rachel first met; and he sold drugs throughout high school. That's all he knew. That's all he wanted to know. Rachel looked past his street mentality and saw potential in him at an early age; at least she thought she could mold him into the man she wanted. What she failed to realize is that a person is going to be who they want to be unless they choose different.

After Rachel returned from China, she discovered the unthinkable. Curtis had begun using his own product and he was the father of two other children, by two different women. Both women were in their third trimester before Rachel even left the country.

She was devastated, nonetheless she hadn't fallen out of love with her husband and she took her wedding vows serious. Not only did she want to preserve her marriage for social and political status; according to her mother and the good book, their marriage had been instituted and ordained by God. *Only death was supposed to tear us apart.* She did all she could to rehabilitate him, as well as help him with his illegitimate kids who she secretly despised. Even though it wasn't the children's fault, she hated the idea of him having children with not one, but two different women. Every time his children stepped foot into their home, Rachel became literally sick. She wasn't very religious, but every day she prayed to God, asking him to remove those feelings from her heart and the hateful thoughts from her mind.

She was a strong woman. Curtis Jones knew he had someone special because it takes a special person to understand and deal with all that he had imposed on her. Two years had passed, Curtis had been sober and Rachel was finally adjusting to her stepchildren. Just as things appeared to be getting back to normal, suddenly Rachel was struck with that feeling in her gut; that feeling of intuition that most women get when things seem to be right, but knowing something was definitely going on. Every now and then Rachel would check her husband's voicemail without his knowledge. Somehow she was able to crack his code. It's true what they say, when a person goes looking for something, they are sure to find it.

It was a beautiful afternoon in May. The Jones family had reservations at Mancy's Steakhouse. Rachel decided to check her husband's voicemail while he was out. Leah, one of the "baby mommas" was on the voicemail as usual, but this message was different. She claimed she was pregnant again, with what would be Curtis' fifth child; the third outside of their marriage. Apparently these two never stopped sleeping together. Rachel felt so betrayed after having his back through everything. *Maybe she isn't really pregnant. Perhaps she's just yearning for some extra attention. Still, obviously he's doing more than picking up and dropping off their son for her to even leave a message like this on his phone. Okay, think Rachel, think.* Rachel decided to send the kids to her parents for the weekend, because only God knew what she planned on doing to him.

She went along with their dinner plans minus the children. She hadn't worn her hair down in a while so she decided to curl it cute, the way Mr. Jones liked it. She put on the sexiest dress she could find in her closet, accessorizing from head to toe. Just as she smeared on her MAC lip-gloss, she heard the front door open. Looking in the mirror, she blew herself a kiss and whispered, "show time."

"Rachel, baby! Is my beautiful family ready to go out and have a nice dinner?" Curtis called out as he walked through the house. He found his wife in the bedroom. Suddenly he remembered how fine she was. Standing in the doorway he was completely mesmerized by her appearance. Holding a dozen roses in his hand, he was speechless for the first time in a long time.

Rachel could feel a knot growing in her throat, knowing if she didn't swallow it quickly; tears would flow from her eyes like water in Lake Erie. "The kids are over my parents' house. I thought you and I needed some alone time. It's going to be a long night, if you know what I mean." She was convincing. Had it not been for her large investment banking company, she could have easily been a Hollywood actress.

"These are for you." He handed his wife the beautiful array of flowers. *Screw you and your flowers* is all Rachel could think. Instead of saying what she felt, she swallowed the knot in her throat again and reached for the roses. Putting a fake smile on her face, she sniffed the bouquet with her cute little squirrel nose and placed them on the dresser behind her. Before she knew it, her husband was kissing her. He gently tossed her on the bed and began sucking her bottom lip. She wanted to vomit in her own mouth at that very moment. She felt so deceived by him.

I should bite down on his lip, like a pit bull and not let go until it falls off. He has some nerve kissing on me with the same lips he used to kiss Leah and Tara. Her thoughts were racing all over the place as she lay on the bed, imagining the things he did to the other women. All the thoughts and feelings she had recently overcome were all coming back. "Babe, we're going to be late. Trust me dessert is later." Finally he stopped. She felt so violated by his touch.

He helped his wife up from the bed and began stroking her jet black hair in an effort to put it back in place. Again she felt disgusted by his touch. She followed her husband down the stairs and thought about pushing him the rest of the way down. *Okay, okay stop.* She silently thought to herself. *Lord please control my emotions, I really don't want to hurt him. Please God console me.* She took a deep breath and promised herself she would remain calm.

They valet parked Curtis' Infiniti SUV, which was a gift from his wife, and were escorted to their favorite table. Rachel ordered her usual feast of lobster and shrimp, while Curtis sank his teeth into a medium rare steak. Rachel was not a fan of red meat, but she couldn't seem to break her husband from that habit; amongst other things. She loved to drink wine and since tonight would be a rare occasion, she ordered a bottle of Chateau Haut Brion for the two of them. They sipped on wine and laughed for hours before they departed the restaurant. She had such a good time that she almost forgot to be pissed off.

The ride home was silent and seemed to be longer than usual. Curtis kept one hand on the steering wheel and placed the other on his wife's thigh. His touch almost felt good to Rachel. It was always like that; he would mess up followed by doing something sweet, reminding Rachel of how much she truly loved him, which led to forgiveness. This man sold drugs, stole from his wife, became a crack head, cheated, had her paying child support for kids that he fathered outside of their marriage and all she knew how to do was love and forgive him. Everyone in the city of Toledo considered her to be one of the bossiest ladies in town, everyone except for herself. The truth was this beautiful intelligent woman had low self-esteem. She thought since her husband cheated so much and treated her wrong, obviously there had to be something wrong with her.

Curtis pulled his SUV into the three car garage and placed the car in park. Reclining his seat back, he motioned for his wife to climb on top of him. He started kissing her and she liked it. The red wine had temporarily changed her mood. They made out in the car like they used to do when they were in high school. "Let's go inside." She whispered into her husband's ear. She stripped nude in the kitchen and made her husband chase her up to the bedroom.

She was back to loving him as he caressed her in his arms. "Baby." He muttered in between kissing his wife. "I love you so much." He continued kissing her while peering in her eyes. "I'll never do anything to ever hurt you again or jeopardize losing what we have." At that instant she became outraged, remembering Leah was once again pregnant by her husband. The nerve of him to let those lies fall off his lips so loosely.

"I know baby." She said lying back to her deceiving husband. "Lay back; I want to try something different tonight." Following his wife's command he was excited about the element of surprise. Rachel got up to find something to tie up her husband. All kinds of thoughts were running through her head. "I'll be back in a moment." She called out to her husband as she gathered scarves and tape.

She crawled back in the bed and began kissing her husband slowly and sensually. The lifetime movies that she watched on Saturday mornings would finally pay off. She tied his hands above his head and connected them to the headboard. Thinking about how betrayed and hustled she felt, she tied a scarf around his ankles and connected them to the footboard as she muttered, "So you say you'll never hurt me or jeopardize us again?" He shook his head no, gazing at his wife with his bedroom eyes. She made sure the scarves were extra tight so that his 200 pound body couldn't break free. Ripping a thick piece of tape, she kissed his lips once more and sealed his lips with the tape.

She began crying hysterically. Curtis looked at his wife with a puzzled look, not understanding how she could go from being turned on to a psycho in a matter of seconds. "Why is—I mean how is Leah pregnant by you again?" Her voice was cracking. Curtis couldn't respond. His demeanor converted from being puzzled to being afraid. His eyes began to water not because he regretted what he did; he feared what his wife was going to do to him. She went to the closet and grabbed their pistol from the box off the shelf. She also grabbed a leather belt and stood back over her husband.

She began to stroke the side of his face with the loaded gun. She began to pray, asking God to forgive her for her premeditated thoughts. She started laughing. "You probably think I'm going to kill you. Really, I should. I could probably get off easily by claiming temporary insanity. But the way I see it, I have invested too much into you, too much into us and your sorry ass isn't even worth a bullet!" She laughed some more until her laughter turned into an uncontrollable cry. "You know Curtis; I'm sick and tired of being sick and tired. Do you like to see me cry? Answer me!" He shook his head no. "Am I not pretty enough? What is it Curt? You still act like we are in high school. Baby, when are you going to change?" Drilling him with question after question, knowing he couldn't give a verbal response being that his lips were bind together with tape, what she really wanted was for him to listen. Rachel wanted Curtis to feel all the pain he brought to her.

"Aaaahhhhhhhhhhhh!" Rachel screamed to the top of her lungs.

She was crying so hard that mucus ran from her nostrils to the top of her lip. Her mascara was running and beads of sweat were dripping profusely from her forehead. "You're a crack head! You mean to tell me I'm losing my mind over a damn dope fiend. You're rehabilitated my ass, once a user, always a user!" As sweet as Rachel was, she could be raw when she reached her breaking point. She took the belt she had been holding in her hand and struck him across his chest. Curtis wanted to scream, but Rachel was clever in making sure he couldn't. She struck him repeatedly until her forearm began to ache.

"I tried to be patient with you, even when you weren't patient with yourself! And this is the thanks I get? You don't even have the decency to protect yourself or me. What if you would have brought me back a disease?" Tears rolled down Curtis' cheek. *Is he remorseful? Nah he's just a sorry excuse for a man.* It was evident that she was angry because this woman said some things she wouldn't have even said to her worst enemy. "I hate you! I hate you Curtis Anthony Jones with a passion. Why Curtis? How could you do this to meeeeeeeeeeeeee?" I love you and it hurts." She buried her face in her husband's half beaten chest. She cried on him, allowing her tears to wash away the pain she had afflicted on him. She didn't hate him. Truthfully he had been the only man she knew on a romantic level, the only man she had ever loved and trusted besides her father.

He knew he had someone special, but he continued to hurt her without a warning or a reason. He wanted to hold his wife and comfort her and she wanted him to just as much, but he was tied up and Rachel wasn't ready to let him loose. He needed to suffer. Although Curtis was strong enough to break free from his bondage, a part of him wanted to lie there, taking whatever his wife dished out. He felt he may have deserved some physical abuse, for all the emotional and mental abuse he put on Rachel. She was strong enough to take it, so why shouldn't he?

She lay on her husband's chest trying to pretend none of this had taken place. She tried to pretend Leah wasn't pregnant, nor had she or Tara ever been pregnant by her husband. The more she pretended the more real it became to her. Once again she went into a rage. "Aaaahhhhhhhhhhhhh!" Her scream pierced her husband's eardrum. "I hate you so much. Get your things—better yet, since I bought everything you ain't taking shit! Leave your, well, my car, in the garage and get out! Go be with Leah and her four children who were all conceived by different men!" Curtis was crying. He didn't want to lose his wife or the lifestyle he was accustomed to.

"You wanna go from sugar to shit, well be my guest Curtis. Do you honestly think I can't find a man; one who will treat me right and appreciate the woman I am. Well, you are sadly mistaken. I'm tired Curt. I look at our children and I am beginning to believe they are tired too. Christina and CJ barely interact with you when you're around." She started crying again. Looking at the clock on the dresser she realized it was 1:00 am, meaning she had been tormenting her husband for over two hours. Rachel took the belt and whacked her husband a few more times. She struck him across his face and the rest of his body. She was weary and suddenly had a banging headache.

"I hate you Curtis." She was so weak she could only whisper. "After all we've been through . . . . I can't go through a second longer." Taking her ring off and placing it on her husband's chest, she looked at him and whispered, "I want a divorce." That was her breaking point. She never asked for a divorce. "Screw you Curtis!" She attempted to yell but her throat was a mess. "Screw you, your bastard children and their mothers. Better yet, screw your mother for a bringing a monster like you into this world!" At that point Rachel felt ashamed. She never conducted herself in such a manner, not even when she was provoked by Leah on several occasions. She placed her face in her hands and wept. She was so embarrassed. Crawling into the bed next to her husband who was still tied up, she placed her head on his chest, crying herself to sleep.

Curtis had no choice but to lay next to his wife, as she snored in her sleep. He silently prayed that she would forgive him once more. This time he was really going to change. He thought about asking Leah to abort the unborn child. *Maybe the baby's not even mine. I'm not with her twenty-four seven. Besides, it took her a few blood tests to figure out who the fathers were of her first two children. Damn, I really messed up this time. I'm tired of hurting my wife. Lord, please forgive me and I pray my wife forgives, again.* Tears streamed down his face. Finally he fell asleep next to his temporary deranged wife. Both of them slept uneasy, wondering what the day would bring.

Rachel was awakened by the sound of her cell phone vibrating on the night stand. She pretended as if she didn't hear it, trying to steal a few more minutes of sleep. The vibration continued, forcing her to roll over and look at the clock. It was nine in the morning. She turned back over and looked at her husband. She almost chuckled seeing that he was still tied to the bed. Rachel quickly remembered what happened last night was far from a laughing matter. Finally she answered the phone. "Hello?"

"Hey girl, I just wanted to confirm our date for today." It was her cousin Tausha, who was always excited about the times they shared together.

Do I really want to go outside today? I just want to hide from the world for as long as I can. Before she could give it any further thought she was giving her cousin confirmation. "I wouldn't miss it for anything in the world." Rachel really didn't want to be bothered, but she knew if she could talk to anyone about anything without being judged, it was her cousin. "Is it possible for you to pick me up?"

"Sure can hon. I'll see you at twelve!" Tausha exclaimed, hanging up the phone. Rachel hopped out of the bed and marched into the master bathroom to brush her teeth and wash her face. She looked in the mirror and wasn't very pleased with the reflection. Mascara was smeared across her face and her eyes were coated with crust. Wishing she could forget about what happened last night, she wiped her face with a warm towel. She was tired of crying and decided not to shed another tear for Curtis; at least not in front of him. Almost frightened to untie her husband, she crept back into the bedroom and stood over him. Curtis abused his wife in a number of ways, but he never laid his hands on her. Drool was seeping from underneath the tape that kept his mouth sealed. *I must have done a number on him.* Curtis had a cut on his right eyebrow and his chest was a bluish-purple color. His muscle toned thighs and legs also possessed evidence of physical abuse.

Ironically, Mrs. Jones no longer felt the remorse or embarrassment that she felt last night. Oddly enough, she felt liberated and that justice had prevailed for all women who had been mistreated by their mate. She untied him and then ripped the tape from his mouth. His wrists and ankles were also black-and-blue. He reached up to hug his wife, but she quickly rejected him. "Curtis Jones, please don't say anything. As a matter of fact, there is nothing you can say to make me change my mind. I want you out of my house and please don't take any of my belongings. Just leave. I'll be calling my lawyer." She talked in a stern voice. She took a deep breath, pausing for moment. Looking her husband square in the eye with a look that wasn't familiar to him, she slowly, but firmly said, "Yes, I want a divorce. Until it is finalized, I don't think the children should be around you. It would only confuse matters more." Folding her arms she glared at him as if to say, *try me, I dare you!*

Curtis was sobbing like a baby, knowing there was nothing he could say or do to win Rachel over. He put on a pair of sweats and sneakers, not even attempting to take anything else per his wife's request. He wanted to kiss his wife; instead he put his head down and walked away. Rachel ran to the window and watched her husband leave. She stared out the window until she could no longer see him. *Oh well he probably just had one of those baby mommas pick him up at the corner. Lord knows his lazy behind ain't walking too far.*

She took a long sigh and moved down to the kitchen to eat some breakfast. Rachel was extremely health conscious. She nibbled on a cup of fruit and scrambled egg whites. After reading the morning paper she skipped into the family room and turned on the radio. One sad love song after another aired over the radio. Finally, one song caught her attention; "Mistreated," by Shawn Kane. The song basically told her she didn't have to accept defeat and to get up and get herself together. Shawn's voice was both sexy and soothing to Rachel, motivating her to fix herself up and prepare for a day of fun with her cousin.

In the shower, she tried to wash away all the pain Curtis caused, as well as the shame she felt for trying to beat some sense into him the night prior. *It's a thin line between love and being someone's fool.* Rachel thought about her life with Curtis as she lathered soap over her body. She dried off and slipped into her soft terry cloth robe. "Fix yourself up, call your girls up . . ." She began singing the lyrics to "Mistreated" as she made up her face. Rachel believed even though a person was going through something, they didn't necessarily have to look the part. Putting her long hair up into a cute ponytail, she threw on her Bebe jeans and a tank top, dressing her outfit up with a cute scarf and big earrings.

Just as she slipped into her shoes, she heard tires screeching into her driveway. *That must be Tausha, she drives likes she got her license out of a cereal box.* Rachel raced down the stairs and out of the front door. "Hey sweetie, how are you?" Tausha greeted her cousin as she opened the passenger door. "Don't you look cute? You know I thought you weren't coming for real, you know how you being playing all the time." Rachel smiled at her cousin as she entered the Pontiac G6. "Ooh, this is my song!" Tausha started bouncing around in her seat as she turned up the radio and reversed out of the driveway. Rachel shook her head and gazed out of the window.

Mrs. Jones was beginning to worry about her husband's whereabouts. *I wonder who he's with. Should I let him come back? I've invested too many years to just throw them all away. But I'm tired of fighting for his love that should be unconditional.* Curtis was her first in everything; apparently she just wasn't enough for him. Tears rolled down her cheeks as she looked out the window and thought about her husband. "I kicked Curtis out this morning. Yeah and uh, Leah's pregnant again, by Curtis."

"What?" Tausha screeched as she gripped the steering wheel tighter. A look of disgust was painted all over her face. She shook her head repeatedly and turned down the music. "You know what, forget him. I just feel bad because I'm the one who convinced you into giving his no-good behind another chance. I'm so sorry and I'm going to be here for you. He doesn't deserve you, he deserves someone like Leah, he ain't worth nothing and neither is she! As a matter of fact, what's her address I'm gonna whip her ass for you." Tausha was crazy like that and always felt compelled to stand up for her cousin, even if it meant getting a little violent.

Rachel reached into her purse and pulled out a pack of tissues. She started to laugh through her tears at her cousin, almost wishing she hadn't told her. "Tausha, you are crazy."

"Nah sweetie, I'm serious. And if you got a little serious from time to time, Curtis wouldn't walk all over you. You are too good of a person . . ." Tausha was cut off by her cousin.

"Yeah, but real things still happen to good people. It's not just Leah's fault, Curtis just isn't ready to change. I refuse to do anything or allow you to do anything crazy; it's so not worth it. I'll get through this. Now let's hurry up and get to Massage Expo!" Rachel pulled herself together. She was good at keeping a level head or putting up a good front rather. *I guess I shouldn't tell her that I did get a little crazy on him last night.* The two ladies got massages, pedicures, and facials. They shopped until they were ready to drop and then Tausha took Rachel to pick up her children.

Once in the house Rachel cuddled up with her kids and explained to them that their father would be away for awhile. Christina was sharp and from the look she gave her mom, she knew her dad had messed up again. She held her mother's hand and the three of them watched Cartoon Network until it was time for bed.

Rachel put her children to bed and phoned her personal assistant to let her know she would be taking the rest of the week off. She wanted some time alone. No matter how much she tried telling herself she was going to be okay, the truth was, her heart was aching and it felt as if someone had cut off her oxygen. *I guess that's what happens when you allow a person to drive you insane, not enough oxygen can reach your brain.*

Chapter Two

Straddling the Fence

Tossing and turning in the bed, Rachel couldn't help but to think about Curtis. She called his phone five times and did not get an answer. She was actually worried about her husband and was hoping nothing bad happened to him. She dozed off for a few hours and then woke up to the sound of the wind beating on the window. It was 2:00 am. She looked at her cell phone to see if she had any missed calls; preferably from her husband. *Not a single call.* She decided to try his phone again. Finally, the other end picked up. A soft voice answered the phone. "Hello?" It was not her husband, it was . . .

"Leah? Put my husband on the phone right now!" Rachel was pissed and hurt simultaneously.

"I would, but he's sleep. By the way, you woke me and our baby up!" Leah retorted as she hung up on Rachel.

Rachel was fuming. She wanted to call her cousin to console her, but decided that it might be a bad idea. She knew Tausha wasn't wrapped too tight and the both of them would end up behind bars. She thought about praying, but couldn't find what she thought would be an appropriate prayer. Instead she hugged Curtis' pillow, smelling the residue of his cologne and cried herself to sleep.

She found peace right before daybreak, which didn't last for long. She was awakened by her kids singing, "Momma, we're hungry." Rachel didn't have the energy to move; sadness and a broken heart had her physically and mentally drained. Christina studied her mother and knew something was wrong. "Mommy you can lay down. I'll make us some cereal and juice. I'm a big girl, okay mommy? Come on CJ. Let mommy rest." Christina was so mature to only be six years old.

"Okay baby. Thank you. I love you guys so much." Rachel uttered to her children as they walked out of her room. She knew she had to regain her focus at least for her children's sake. She decided to call her husband again. She was determined to make it work and keep her family together. Realizing she had to take the bad with the good, because she couldn't allow someone else to be with him. She heard the other end pick up and decided to wait until she knew who it was before she spoke.

"What Rachel! You put me out, remember? Now that I'm with my other family, you want to keep calling me! What is it, and speak fast because you have me taking time away from them."

"What do you mean *your other family*?" Rachel couldn't suppress her tears. "You have some nerve talking to me like that! I am your wife!" Her emotions got the best of her and she broke down. She could hear Leah in the background laughing; it was obvious he had Rachel on speaker phone, making a mockery of her feelings. She was crushed. *How could he be so heartless?* She cried until she felt as if she could no longer breathe. She could not resist it any longer. She picked up the phone and dialed her cousin's number.

Her cousin kept yelling, "Hello!" Rachel couldn't reply; all she could do was cry. "I'll be there in ten minutes!" Tausha yelled through the phone and hung up.

It was more like six and half minutes before Tausha arrived. Rachel managed to drag herself out of the bed and down the stairs to let her cousin in the house. "Sorry hon, Melissa was in the car with me when you called and I needed to get over here right away." Tausha apologized to her cousin for bringing an outsider around at a time like this.

Rachel didn't care; she just rested her head on her cousin's shoulder and cried. Tausha fed her little cousins and bathed them. Once she had seen after them she finished consoling her cousin. Tausha always believed in making children a first priority; no matter what was going on. Rachel continued crying as she told her cousin about Curtis' behavior.

After about thirty minutes Melissa interrupted the two cousins. "Excuse me Rach, I don't mean to pry or anything, I was wondering if you had a church home?" Rachel sniffled and shook her head no. "Well maybe you can come to church with me next week, my pastor's young and you'll be able to relate to the messages he delivers."

"Sure Melissa. I need to be in somebody's church. That's where I messed up. They say a family who prays together, stays together. But I guess that's my fault." Rachel said, sounding sorry for herself.

"God never puts more on us than what we can bear. If He brought you to it, please believe He'll bring you through it. By the way, my pastor is single and fine. Everybody wants to get with Pastor Jackson, Umm, with his fine self!" Melissa went from being comforting to comical.

"Well now that we got that out of the way, Rach please get up and brush your teeth! I didn't want to tell you because you were crying and going through it, but your breath is not the best!" Tausha was funny like that, she made sure a situation was under control and then she'd tell you about yourself.

"Sorry cousin." Rachel said half laughing and covering her mouth with her hand.

"Don't be sorry, be careful!" That was Tausha's favorite line. The three women laughed hysterically.

After the visit from her cousin, Rachel attempted to hold it together, even though she was suffering from a busted heart. The days grew long for Ms. Jones during her hiatus from work. Her children were at school and her husband was missing in action. Calling him would only make matters worse, so she did everything in her power not to. Had it not been for her children, Mrs. Jones would have stayed in bed every day—all day. If Christina wasn't such an honest child, telling her mother, "Mommy, you look a mess!" She probably would have kept on the same clothes without even fixing her hair.

She was almost excited about going to church on Sunday. Rachel was a believer, but the only time her family attended service was on Easter Sunday and Mother's day. CJ and Christina usually went to church with her parents if they were with them on the weekends. As a child, Rachel went to Church with her parents at least three times per week. Even though she had steered away from going, she always remembered that feeling of comfort. Her mom would often say, "Rachel, you are blessed and I'm proud of you. You better know where your help comes from. The Lord gave you all of this and you better believe he can take it away!" Rachel didn't take what her mother said for granted; she just wasn't ready to play church. Somehow her parents found out about what she was going through and when Friday came around, they decided it was best for the children to spend the entire weekend with them. She loved her babies, but she couldn't agree more with her parents. She didn't want them to see her suffering.

She stayed in the house Friday, but on Saturday Tausha convinced her to get out and live a little. They went to Club Print in downtown Toledo. Rachel hadn't been out in years and it showed. She danced to every song the DJ played. It was apparent that she was still a hot commodity, because every direction she turned some brotha was trying to get her number or give his to her. Rachel wasn't impressed, she just smiled out of politeness and kept grooving to the music. Sitting at the bar, she sipped on a glass of Nuvo with cherries. She looked at her ring finger only to remember she had taken her ring off and gave it to her husband. *He probably took it the pawn shop by now.* "Hey Taush, I've had enough fun for one night. Let's go. I promised Melissa I would meet her at church in the morning." She almost felt bad for going out, and then going to church, but it was almost a social norm. The majority of the people in the club would be heading to Sunday morning service afterwards.

Once at home, Rachel was feeling a little buzz from the alcohol and decided to call Curtis. Surprisingly he answered his phone. "Babe, come home. I miss you." The effects of alcohol bring out one's true feelings. Curtis agreed and within twenty minutes he pulled into his wife's driveway with Leah's loud Ford Escort. Rachel didn't even get upset; she just wanted her husband there. In the morning she knew she could blame it on the alcohol.

Curtis reeked of smoke and cheap liquor. While lying in her husband's arms, she realized she no longer wanted him there. His touch didn't feel right; his odor wasn't even the same. She felt numb, but instead of kicking him out right away, she decided to allow him to stay until morning. "I'm sorry Rach. I miss my family." Rachel rolled her eyes in the dark and nodded her head to Curtis' half heartfelt statement. They slept in each other's arms until morning.

The sunlight snuck in through the blinds, smacking the Jones' in their face. Curtis gripped his wife tighter as if to say, *I'm never letting you go again.* His thoughts were quickly interrupted when the phone and the alarm clock sounded off in chorus. Rachel rolled over and hit the snooze, ignoring the phone. She curled back under her husband to catch a few more minutes of shut eye.

The phone started ringing again. Rachel groaned, snatching the phone off the hook. She held the receiver to her ear without saying a word.

"Hello! Hello? Rachel?" It was Leah's loud and obnoxious voice. Rachel remained silent, giving Leah the opportunity to speak. "I'm not trying to be rude or nuthin', but Curtis has my car and I gotta take one of my kids to their dad's house so she can get some shoes! If he don't bring my car, I'm gonna report it stolen and send the police to your house!"

Rachel was livid. *I don't have time for this ghetto mess.* Hearing Leah's voice was so unnerving. "Here you go Curtis." Rachel slapped him in his head with the phone and leaped out of the bed. She could hear Leah yelling through the phone. "The devil is a lie." She spoke to herself as she prepared her clothes for church.

Once Curtis hung up the phone, he got out of the bed and came sniffing after his wife like a sad puppy. Rachel knew it was over. Dealing with ghetto drama was not her forte. "Look Curtis." Rachel sighed. She was poised and had a stern look on her face. Curtis knew the look wasn't good. "Just take your clothes and go. I have no use for your belongings and I'm done trying to prove a point. I shouldn't have to prove anything to you; I'm not the one who got caught with my pants down. I can't live like this. You are my husband, but I feel like we're creeping. Something's definitely wrong with this picture. Your girlfriend's car is parked in my driveway and she's calling my home making threats. It's over baby, I know for a fact I can't do this; I won't do this. Take as much time as you need to gather your things, I have to get ready for church." She gave him a hug and kissed him on the cheek. A feeling of relief rose up inside of Rachel. Feeling as though she conquered a giant or a monster, she smiled at her husband.

Curtis packed his belongings in a hasty manner. Without saying goodbye, he left. Rachel could hear the car pull away from her house. Refusing to watch him depart like before, she continued getting dressed.

Trying to get into the spirit, Rachel let the sound of gospel blast through the speakers of her Mercedes as she drove to church. It was very rare that she traveled to Toledo's north side, so she took mental notes of all the landmarks. As she cruised down Velmont Street, she prayed for emotional healing and hoped the pastor would touch on her situation in his sermon. *I need a healing for my soul.*

She pulled in the parking lot belonging to St. Mary's Church. She combed through her hair with her fingers, tugged on her skirt and strutted into the ancient building. Clutching her Bible underneath her arm, she started to perspire as she walked past the members of the church. Her nerves kicked in. She felt as if everyone was looking at her; as if she didn't belong in the Lord's house. Positioning herself in a pew directly behind Melissa, she tapped her on the shoulder and whispered, "Hey girl, I made it." Melissa turned around and gave her a huge smile.

Melissa was a very pretty lady who possessed a style of her own. She was thick and knew how to embrace her thickness. She'd been married twice, and had no children. Being a voluptuous woman, she often wore blouses that revealed a lot of cleavage. Rachel was surprised that her friend's boobs were popping out in the sanctuary. Rachel sat back and enjoyed the praise and worship. She wasn't one to do all the hooting and hollering, but she did worship. A side door opened and she noticed a tall slender man wearing glasses enter into the pulpit. He began to sing with the choir. His voice was amazing. When the song was over Rachel noticed she was crying, because the song was so encouraging and it was speaking directly to her circumstance.

Taking his Bible and pushing his spectacles from the brim of his nose, he started speaking and reading some announcements. "Before I bring forth the word, I would like to say it is good to see all of you in the house of the Lord on this day. If there be any visitors, please stand and introduce yourself." His voice was low and raspy. He looked directly at Rachel as if to say, *stand up; I know you are not a member.*

Rachel stood up and looked around. No one else was standing; therefore it was obvious she was the only one visiting. Clearing her throat and half looking at the ground, she spoke in an innocent girlish tone. "Good morning, I'm Rachel Jones and I'm visiting with my friend Melissa Mitchell. I don't have a church home, but I'm here today." She sat down feeling silly because she really didn't know how to address the congregation. Melissa turned around and winked at her as if to say *relax.*

Pastor Christopher Jackson looked Rachel dead in her eyes and said, "Well on behalf of St. Mary's, we are glad that you are here and we hope that you will keep coming." Rachel smiled and nodded her head. He went on to preach from the book of Job. Rachel took notes so that she could study throughout the week. She really enjoyed the sermon. For the first time she felt as if she was in a church that correlated their teachings with real life. She knew she would come again.

After he was done preaching, he laid hands on a few people and prayed over them. Once dismissed, he encouraged everyone to meet and greet with one another. Rachel hugged Melissa. "Thanks for inviting me. I really needed this and I'll be back next Sunday." She left the sanctuary without greeting any of the other members. Service was so invigorating for Rachel. Feeling like a new creature, she cruised away from St. Mary's and headed to her parents' house.

Her parents lived in the same house for the past thirty years. Her grandfather and great-uncles built it with their bare hands. They had it renovated ten years ago, but vowed they would never leave. Rachel's parents were both retired. Her mom had been a nurse and her dad a dentist. Her parents had the most beautiful relationship; if they ever had any problems it was never evident. Mr. Belmont treated his wife like a queen. Rachel wished that Curtis was half the man her father was.

When she pulled down Sycamore Road, she spotted her children playing in the yard with her mother. There were so many toys in the front lawn; it looked as though they were planning a yard sale. Rachel was glowing. She kept holding on to the scripture she had in her heart. *Things can only go up from here,* she told herself.

"Christina, CJ. Come here and give your mommy a hug and a kiss." They ran to their mom with excitement in their eyes. Rachel loved her children and sometimes regretted the time she spent away from them to promote her business. To make up for lost time, she would often shower them with expensive unnecessary gifts. She would often joke on how she felt like she was the female version of a baby daddy; the type of dad that only showed his face on holidays, birthdays and blew lots of money on those specific occasions.

She told her mom about her church experience and how Melissa had a secret crush on the reverend. Her mom was happy to see her daughter smiling. "It doesn't matter where you go Rach, as long as you go. A lot of folks say church is in their heart and not in a building. I agree, but I still believe you need that fellowship and that covering. So how are you feeling about everything else?" Her mom was referring to the situation with Curtis.

"You know Mommy, I can't pretend as if I'm not hurt behind all this . . . . I don't hate my husband and I'm willing to forgive, but I'm tired and I've had enough. I'm calling my lawyer in the morning and I'm filing for divorce." Rachel could tell her mother anything; they were best friends in a sense.

"Rach, you are strong and brave and I'm proud of you. I try to stay out of your business because I know you are wise enough to make your own decisions. However, as a mother, when you're hurt, I feel your pain. If you need anything, your father and I are here for you and our grandbabies." She squeezed her daughter's hand and invited her in for a home cooked Sunday meal.

Rachel sat down with her parents and children, laughing and reminiscing about old times. She and the kids skipped dessert due to the time. Wanting to get the children and herself prepared for a fresh Monday morning, she thanked her parents and headed off.

Before putting her kids to bed she prayed with them and read them a bedtime story. While tucking Christina in, her daughter looked up at her with her big bright eyes and said, "Mom, can I talk to you about something?"

Rachel braced herself. *Oh no. She's going to ask me about Curtis and I'm really not up to talking about him.* She kissed her daughter on the forehead. "Sure baby. What is it?"

"Mommy, I don't like sneaks!" Christina exclaimed in an-almost-grown-woman voice.

Is she referring to her father sneaking around? Did she overhear the conversation with Tausha and Melissa? "Sneaks, baby?"

"Yes Mom. You know like the sneak that tricked Eve into eating the apple! I read it in my promise Bible."

"Oh, you mean snakes? Yes, the serpent did trick Eve." Rachel was relieved she didn't have to discuss her husband and his whereabouts. She busted out into laughter until her stomach started to hurt. Christina didn't find any humor in what she said to her mom and was puzzled by her mother's behavior. Rachel tried explaining to her daughter that she wasn't making fun of her, but Christina being the stubborn child that she was, wasn't buying her mother's story.

The next morning after getting the kids off to school, Rachel stuck to her guns and phoned her lawyer, Mr. Larry Dee. Larry assured Rachel he would take care of everything.

Taking it day by day, she went an entire month without calling or accepting calls from Curtis. She reached a happy point in her life and was practicing self-love. Taking a narcissistic stance, Mrs. Jones was beginning to live her life. She went to church every Sunday and was growing stronger in her faith.

Chapter Three

Just Dinner and a Movie

As time went by, Rachel not only grew in her faith, but she had become a better mother. Since it was summer time, she conducted more business outside of Ohio. Instead of leaving her children with her parents as usual, she hired a nanny to travel with her. Curtis had been served his divorce papers and their legal split would be finalized by the end of July. He was so bitter that the judge did not award him alimony or any type of spousal support; he refused to see Christina and Curtis Jr. He had the audacity to say he didn't think they were really his children and demanded a DNA test. Even his bitterness and ignorance couldn't bring Rachel down. Her income had nearly tripled. She believed that her new found relationship with the Lord had a major impact on her business.

While on a business trip in Miami, she received a surprise phone call. Rachel studied the number flashing across her cell phone. Thinking it could be Curtis with redundant drama, she was reluctant about answering the phone.

"Hello?" She held her breath and waited for a response.

"Hello, Mrs. Jones or shall I say Ms. Jones? How are you?" The voice on the phone was raspy and low. She immediately recognized the caller.

"I'm well, thank you." Rachel wasn't sure what this call was in reference to and she was certain that she paid her membership dues before she left.

"This is Christopher Jackson." His voice would have almost been sexy to Ms. Jones, had it not been for his title.

"Oh, hey Pastor." Rachel pretended that she didn't already know it was him.

There was silence for a brief moment followed by a chuckle. "Your voice is so adorable. Please call me Chris; I'm not calling as Pastor right now."

Rachel took the phone away from her hear and quickly examined the number again. She wanted to be sure this wasn't a prank call. Not knowing how to respond or what he could possibly want, she cleared her throat three times before saying anything. *If you're not calling as Pastor Jackson, then who are you? I'm confused. Okay Rachel, get your thoughts together.* "Um-okay, Pastor, I mean Chris." It sounded weird to her using his first name as if they were acquaintances.

He chuckled once again and then in a Barry-Whitish tone he said, "I heard about your divorce and I just wanted to check on you. How are you holding up?"

Melissa can't hold water sometimes. She must have opened her big mouth and told him. "Oh everything is fine Pastor, I mean Chris. Sorry. I'm going to have to try and get used to being on a first name basis with you." She went on to tell him how she really loved being a member of St. Mary's and how much she was growing in her faith. They talked for nearly thirty minutes. Rachel had to admit, talking to him was very therapeutic.

Without warning, Pastor Jackson asked Rachel an unexpected inquiry. "So, when are you going to allow me to take you out?"

There was a long silence. Rachel was flabbergasted. It wasn't too many occasions that she was made to be speechless. All kinds of thoughts raced through her head. She felt both flattered and hesitant. *Like a date? No, maybe it's totally innocent and a part of the new member orientation. And what if it is a date? Melissa would be so upset with me. She is madly in love with Pastor Jackson. What kind of friend would I be if I just stepped on her toes?*

"Did I say something wrong?" Pastor Jackson asked in an apologetic tone.

He is fine. Rachel thought and then quickly reminded herself that her friend possessed that same thought. "No Chris, not at all. Did you mean like out or like out-out?" Rachel felt stupid. She knew the way she phrased that was all jacked up. "I mean . . . ."

Seeing how she was drowning in her thoughts, he chimed in and rescued her. "Just like dinner and a movie. If I'm overstepping my boundaries, I apologize."

Rachel noticed he was direct and sweet. She sort of liked that. Feeling tense and school girlish, she was finally able to give a straight answer. "Dinner and movie is fine, Chris." She did it. She was able to call him by his first name and accept his invitation. Grinning from ear to ear she relaxed and continued to talk. "I'm in Florida right now, but I'll be back in about a week."

"Well you enjoy the rest of your trip and please call me when you come back. In the meantime, if you need to talk or need anything, don't hesitate to call." His raspy voice sounded very sincere.

Rachel hung up the phone and plopped down on the bed. She thought about the conversation that had just taken place. *Melissa is going to hate me. But it's not like they were actually dating, she just has a crush on the man. Still I can't help but feel a tad bit guilty. Should I tell her or just keep it to myself?* It had been so long since she'd been on a date. Curtis had been the only man that she had ever been with and now for the first time, since high school, her first date would be with a pastor! Pulling out her laptop, she worked on her power point slides, preparing for her morning briefing. As she pecked away on the keyboard, Pastor Christopher Jackson continued to run through her mind. She felt as if the next chapter of her life was slowly beginning. "Life after Curtis" is what she called it.

The week seemed like it went by extra slow. Rachel didn't mind because she was really enjoying the time with her children. They shopped, played and hung out at Disney Land. This 25 year old newly single mother was learning how to balance work, family and her personal life as a single parent. Ironically the kids didn't ask about their father and she didn't mention him. Perhaps they noticed how much happier their mother was and how much fun they were finally having with her.

On Friday July 26, 2008, the family along with the nanny packed their belongings and headed to the Fort Lauderdale Airport. While waiting on their flight, Rachel looked at her children and at that moment, she realized how beautiful they were. Christina could easily be a model and CJ was a handsome younger version of their father. It was at that very moment, six and half years after giving birth; she realized what it meant to be a mother. It was the most amazing feeling to Rachel.

After two weeks and a three hour return flight, the family arrived at their home. They were exhausted. Once she got her children settled into their beds, she noticed she had a text message. She thought about disregarding it until morning. Rachel had an awesome time with her children and she didn't want a negative message to ruin the rest of her night. *I know it's only Curtis and I can't feed into him right now.* She snuggled underneath her blanket and laid her blackberry next to her. The message indicator continued to flash. Ignoring the message, she turned over on her side and drifted off to sleep. It felt good to sleep in her own bed alone without longing for her ex-husband.

"I love you, you love me, and we're a happy family . . ." The sound of Barney's voice exploded from her flat screen television and woke her up. Her children had made their way into her bedroom and were sitting at the foot of the bed, eating cereal.

"Good morning babies." Rachel greeted the two and lay back down. They smiled at their mom and gave their attention back to Barney. Rolling over, Rachel noticed the message light on her phone was still blinking. Sighing, she picked up her blackberry and pressed the mailbox icon. It read: *Hello Rachel. I enjoyed talking with you. Hope you had a safe return. Are we still on?*

It was Pastor Jackson. That school girl feeling she felt while talking to him on the phone rose up inside of Rachel all over again. Smiling from ear to ear, she texted back: *I apologize for the delay. Yes, we are still on, I'll be free this evening.* She hit the send button and eagerly waited on his response.

Within seconds he replied with: *J Alexander's for dinner at six, followed by a movie. Cool? Do you want me to pick you up?*

Rachel thought long and hard. Pastor or not, she wasn't ready to let any man know where she and her kids lived, just yet. She texted back with: *No, I'll meet you there. I have to drop the kids off at my parents' house.* He agreed and their date was set in stone.

She was so excited! Still, she couldn't help but to think about Melissa. Melissa and she weren't the best of friends. It was rumored that Melissa slept with Curtis a year after he married Rachel. When Rachel confronted her about the alleged affair, Melissa replied with, "I know you through Tausha, so even if I did, I'm not your friend, so why would it matter." She was defensive, but later apologized for the comment. Rachel always kept that comment in the back of her mind, but over the years she came to really love Melissa as a person and even looked at her like the sister she never had. Therefore, if the rumor was true, Rachel was just settling the score. Although she didn't want to look at it that way, being that she really wasn't a vindictive person.

Rachel decided to get out of bed. She wanted to spend some time with her children before dropping them off. They went to Chuckee Cheese and had a blast! She played games and climbed through the tunnels with her children. She was really enjoying this mom thing. They played for hours, ate pizza and snacked on cotton candy. At 2:00 PM, Rachel called it quits. The kids were worn out and she wanted to shower and primp for her date.

"Mom, Dad!" Rachel yelled into her parent's home. She let herself in without knocking. She found her parents sitting in the den. Her mom was knitting a blanket, while her dad watched Golf. It was the PGA tournament and Tiger Woods was in the lead. Kissing her dad on the cheek, she looked at her mom and asked, "Can they stay here tonight? I sort of have a date." She smiled at her mom as if to say, yes-I-said-date.

"Sure Rach, you go out and enjoy yourself." Mrs. Belmont was smiling at her daughter with that inquiring—minds—want—to-know-look on her face. Rachel kissed her children and headed towards the door. "Uh Rachel, hold up. I'll walk you out." Rachel knew her mom just wanted to pry, but she told her almost anything, so she was cool with it. Once outside her mom gave her a hug and a huge grin. "So who is he?" Rachel's mom spoke in a yes-I'm-being-nosey tone.

She hesitated because she didn't know how her mom would react. Figuring her mom would be happy as long as it wasn't Curtis, she mumbled, "My—I mean the Pastor of St. Mary's." Quickly looking away with embarrassment tattooed on her face, she waited for her mom to respond.

Rachel's mom's eyebrows rose to the top of her hairline. "I don't know about that Rach. That seems wicked. He's there to preach not prey on vulnerable women."

Rachel was shocked and in a state of disbelief. "Well Mother, he is a single man. How else do you think they find first ladies? If you think they're appointed to the pastors then you are sadly mistaken." Rachel was always respectful and never talked back, but she was pissed off at her mom for being so judgmental.

"Do not talk to me in that pitch, Rachel Michelle Belmont! I just don't want to see you get hurt. Besides, I thought Melissa had a crush on him." Mrs. Belmont was definitely upset and it showed, being that she used her daughter's middle name and maiden last name. She hadn't done that since Rachel was in high school.

"She does. On the other hand, he's not her man, and he and I aren't creeping around. Mom, I'm not having sex with the man. It's just dinner and a movie."

Mrs. Belmont hugged her daughter once more. "I'm sorry sweetie. I overreacted. I've been in the church for a long time and I've witnessed a lot and heard a lot. But my daughter can definitely hold her own ground; I trust that. Enjoy your date."

Rachel smiled at her mom as if to say thank you. *Okay that was a little weird.*

She left and prepared for her date. Pacing from the front to the back of her large walk-in closet, she didn't have a clue about what she should wear. *Is he going to be in a suit and gator shoes?* She didn't want to overdress, but she certainly couldn't wear Club Print attire. It was a quarter after three and she still needed to shower, plus do hair and makeup. Finally she decided to go with her any-occasion black dress and her favorite sangria BCBG pumps. Accessorizing with the perfect earrings and necklace, she was able to hop in the shower. While showering, Rachel prayed that she wouldn't say anything stupid or show signs of extreme nervousness.

Standing in the tall oval shaped mirror, she checked herself out from head to toe; left to right. She looked amazing. *Okay Rachel. Be cool, calm, and collected. Work it girl!*

She arrived at the restaurant fifteen minutes early and Pastor Jackson was already standing outside. "Damn." Rachel whispered. *He really is fine. Now I see what Melissa's hype is all about.* He was dressed in jeans, a designer button-down and Ferragamo shoes. Rachel felt herself getting nervous as her knees began to shake. Parking the car, she took a few deep breaths to calm her nerves. She strutted up to where he was positioned.

"Hello Rachel. You look wonderful." His long arms stretched from his six-feet, two-inch tall body and wrapped around Rachel.

Returning the hug, she thought about what she wanted to say. *You look and smell amazing.* Pretending to be shy, she just smiled and followed him into the restaurant.

Pastor Jackson ordered a steak, shrimp, rice pilaf and a salad. Rachel played it safe by ordering a salad with a side of grilled chicken and vinaigrette dressing.

"You have the most beautiful eyes." He starred Rachel right in her eyes.

"Thank you." Rachel kept a low tone.

"If I make you feel uncomfortable, please let me know." He paused for a second, giving her an opportunity to respond. Then he went on to say, "So tell me what you thought when I first asked you out?"

The question caught Rachel off guard. "Well." Stopping to take a deep breath and swallowing the excess saliva, Rachel wanted to be sure she chose her words carefully. "I didn't think anything; I figured it was like a new member meeting or something."

"You thought it was a new members' meeting?" He looked at her and started laughing. Rachel starred at him with a smile plastered across her face. "No sweetie, this is not a new members' meeting. Please don't get it twisted, I don't ask my members out; whether they be new or old. From the first day I saw you, I thought—well I still think you are beautiful. I just wanted the opportunity to get to know you. I hope it's not too sudden with your divorce and all."

Rachel leaned back in her chair, thinking about the movie "Waiting to Exhale," she took a deep breath and exhaled. She didn't know what to say. He reached over and placed his giant hand on top of hers. "Uh-sure, I'd like the chance to get to know you too . . . Chris." Melissa flashed through her mind and before she thought about what she was going to say next she blurted out, "Well I don't know. You know my friend Melissa has a thing for you." She attempted to look serious, but couldn't stop smiling at him. He was so fine and manly.

"Melissa who?" He asked with a puzzled look in his eyes. Rachel looked at him with a please-don't-play-dumb-expression. Running his soft manicured hand across her hand, he said, "I hope not. I mean, no, I didn't know that. Melissa is a sweet lady, but she's not my type."

"But she is pretty." Rachel was semi-defending her friend, because she didn't see how Melissa wasn't his type. She was almost offended.

"Yeah, she's nice looking, but she's a little on the big side for me." He widened his eyes to emphasize the word big.

He is a mess. I can't believe we're having this conversation. Rachel shook her head and called him silly. "Well what are you going to do about it?" She felt obligated to her friend and wanted to assure she wasn't stepping on her toes. *Maybe I care more about her than what I should.*

"Do about what? Melissa? I'm not going to do anything. Who am I here with? A man finds the woman; it's not the other way around. I don't like what I see with her clothes on, so I'm definitely not trying to see her with clothes off!" He spoke in a don't-ask-me-about-this-anymore voice.

Rachel was both shocked and satisfied with his response. *So did he ask me out, because he wants to see me with my clothes off?* The waitress returned to the table with their meals. They talked and laughed. Rachel's stomach was in knots from laughing so hard. Pastor Jackson had a sense of humor and personality that was out of this world. After dinner, the two went to see the movie "Jumper" starring Samuel L. Jackson. Rachel cuddled up with the pastor while watching the movie. Feeling as if she knew him forever, she quickly reached a feeling of comfort. He held her small hands during the movie and Rachel felt special.

After the movie was over he walked her to her car. They stood in the parking lot and talked for about 10 minutes. "So what do you think about Pastors?" He was curious as to what she was thinking.

"I didn't think you guys were this fun to hang out with. I thought you only went to church and sat in the house and read your Bibles." Rachel laughed at her own response, although she was half serious.

He smiled at her and patted her on the head as if she was a cute little child. "No, we go out, we have fun within reason. I don't serve a boring God, so why should I live a boring life? I go to Florida often, maybe one day you can join me."

"Perhaps I will." Although the invite seemed to be moving their relationship on a little too fast, Rachel was ready to live her life on a more spontaneous level. It was kind of disturbing that a pastor was making such quick advances and it made her wonder what his motives really were. Yet, she decided not to question him. She just wanted to live in the moment. Rachel smiled at him. Standing on her tiptoes, the five-feet, three-inch tall woman hugged the man who could potentially be her new guy. She didn't want to rush, but at the same time she had never been single or dated anyone outside of Curtis. Was she turning into one of those women who were afraid of being alone? Would she jump from one relationship to the next? Rachel decided not to worry about anything. She hadn't felt like this in awhile. Driving home with the radio off, the chocolate diva reflected over her beautiful evening. While driving, she heard her phone vibrate in her purse. Keeping one hand on the steering wheel, she used the other hand to dig through her purse. It was a text message. She smiled knowing it was Pastor Jackson. At least she hoped it would be him.

She clicked on the message icon button, while trying to watch the road. *This is so illegally dangerous; but I can't resist.* It read: *Hey beautiful. I really had a good time with you. When and where for the next time?*

While smiling, driving and texting like she was sixteen years old all over again, She responded with: *Soon. Let's go to Florida . . . your favorite place.*

He replied with: *Sounds good! Sleep well.* Rachel read his response and tossed her phone in her purse. She picked up her children. Her mom didn't question her, but she could tell her daughter was happy. Rachel got her babies in the house and for the first time in about three years, she allowed her children to share her king size bed with their mom. The little ones said their prayers and drifted off to sleep. Rachel set the alarm clock. She wanted ample time to make Sunday morning breakfast for her kids so they wouldn't be hungry in church. She didn't want these feelings to end, whatever feeling it was.

She nestled up with her sleeping children. She sighed and then whispered to herself, "It was just dinner and a movie."

Chapter Four

Rumor Has It

What Rachel appreciated most about St. Mary's was the "come as you are" dress code. Church wasn't a fashion show at this sanctuary and if it was, then it was not very evident. Every now and then some of the old biddies would have something to say about what certain individuals were wearing. If Pastor Jackson caught wind of this type of talk, he would quickly put them in their places, telling them if they had a problem with the way people dressed, they should take them shopping.

Pastor Jackson had only been preaching at St. Mary's for two years; while most of the members had been there longer than he'd been alive. He was only thirty-six, single, no children, and aside from sermonizing he owned a lucrative business in Chicago. Rumor had it that he was a down low brother and that he and Juan, the church pianist, had been in a secret relationship. They called one another brothers/ roommates. When Pastor Jackson announced to his church in Chicago that he was moving to Ohio to Pastor, Juan packed his belongings and proclaimed he was not moving without him.

Juan was about fourteen years younger than the pastor. His hair was long and relaxed, and he walked with a soft switch. He was dating Karly, a member of the church, who was also a Toledo native. Karly was older than Juan and already had three children. Although she and Juan had been dating for a year, many speculated that she was clandestinely in love with Pastor Jackson; there was church chitchat about them getting together on more than a few occasions.

Melissa had all the juicy church gossip. Rachel never commented on what she heard, she just took it all in as a determining factor on how deep her feelings would get for Pastor Jackson. She couldn't understand how people could say such things about their spiritual leader and still attend church faithfully, week after week. Rachel enjoyed his teaching and decided she wasn't going to allow "he-said-she-said gossip" to deter her from rendering him the proper respect or from coming to church. Although she and the pastor had a date the day before service, she still looked at him as the pastor while sitting in the pews with her children. She was a very private person and knew how to separate her personal affairs from the church.

It was first Sunday, communion was at the altar and all leaders were dressed entirely in white. Pastor Jackson entered the pulpit singing "God Is." His voice could make a person cry and encourage them all at the same time. He was wearing an Italian custom made white robe trimmed in red. The brother stayed sharp.

Melissa tapped Rachel while eyeballing the pastor. "Girl that man is gonna be my husband one day, with his Tyler Perry looking self. The sad part about it is he doesn't even know that he's my man!" He was a spitting image of Tyler Perry. Rachel just looked at Melissa and smiled, knowing if Melissa knew about the date she had with him last night, she would be devastated. Rachel remained focused with her attention directed towards the altar. Melissa kept talking about how fine he was and then she whispered, "Girl, why did my Aunt Marcy who sings in the church choir, tell me the Pastor was a hoe and he's sleeping with every single lady in here. Is she crazy or what?"

Rachel was stunned at the fact that Melissa would even attempt to have such a conversation in church, but at the same time it caught Rachel's attention. She definitely did not want to be another St. Mary's statistic or be a part of the rumor mill. Still she refused to comment. She just shook her head, trying to remain focused. Knowing that she couldn't tell Melissa or anyone for that matter about her new relationship, she told herself that whatever went down between the Pastor and her, it would be their little secret. She noticed that he didn't preach on who should or should not partake in communion. She learned a long time ago that everyone shouldn't participate without first examining their own hearts and repenting. She examined her own heart, repented for beating her ex-husband and the harsh words she spoke to him out of anger and then took communion. Not allowing her kids to partake, she told Christina they would talk about it later.

At the end of service, Rachel greeted the rest of the members. It was the first time she brought her children; a lot of the members didn't even know she had children. For one, she looked a lot younger than her age; and for the most part she kept to herself. Pastor Jackson gave the two children a hug, praying over them. He gave Christina a kiss on the cheek, saying how pretty she was. Suddenly a voice snuck up on Rachel from behind. "Hi Rachel, I'm so glad to see you keep coming back to church." It was Karly; they had known each for years but never really hung out. Rachel gave Karly a hug and departed from the church with her children.

While driving she couldn't help but to think about what Melissa had revealed to her in church regarding her secret friend. *A gay pastor?* She hoped it was only a rumor, she wanted another date. "Momma!" Christina called from the back seat. She was a very inquisitive little girl. Older folks joked about her being on the earth once before. "Is that Pastor related to us?"

Rachel raised her eyebrow not knowing where her six year old was going with her question. "No, baby; he's our pastor. What made you ask that darling?"

"Because he kissed me and he's not my uncle or my daddy. He

shouldn't be kissing me Mommy, he don't know me like that." Christina was a wise little girl who meant exactly what she said.

Rachel smiled at her daughter. "He didn't mean any harm sweetheart, but I'll be sure to let him know." The young mother laughed the rest of the way home. She hadn't cooked a real meal in a long time and decided to make a big dinner for the children. Christina, who ate like a grown woman, while remaining small in size and stature for her age, was excited her mom was actually cooking.

While cooking, she received a text from Pastor Jackson: *You looked really good in church today Ms. Rachel.* Rachel smiled as she read the message, but decided not to respond. She was really digging him and wanted to know if the rumors were true before her feelings grew too deep. *How could I ask him any of those awful questions?* Whether they were going to date or not, she still wanted to be respectful of him and his position. At the same time, she didn't want to become a part of something she would later regret.

After she got the kids fed and settled into bed she decided to call him. She thought it would be best to warn him of all the rumors circulating throughout his congregation. She wasn't a messy person and didn't want him to view her as such. Wanting to be tactful, she rehearsed what she would say prior to dialing his number. As soon as she heard the phone ring, she wanted to hang up, but it was too late.

"Good evening, Rachel. I was just thinking about you. I was wondering when I would have the pleasure to take you out again."

He was so debonair; it was easy to fall for him as quickly as Rachel was. Rachel couldn't bite her tongue any longer. Forgetting about her rehearsal, she blurted out the first thought that came to her mind. "Do you take all the single women out in your church and if not, why me?" Rachel surprised herself, but figured it was too late to swallow what she had just said.

"Wow! I get it. Because of my title and my position, you want to come at me like this? That's why it's so hard for me to date. If I was just a regular dude, you wouldn't question me like this!"

"No-no, that's not it. I'm sorry Chris." She instantly felt bad. Not meaning to hurt his feelings, she decided to tell him all the things that were being said about him. Rachel was drama free and wanted to keep it that way. At the same time she was newly divorced and needed to protect her own heart.

"Well Rachel, let me clarify a few things for you. I'm definitely not gay. Being a single pastor either makes me the poster boy for gays or every single woman in my congregation. That's why I asked you out, I could tell you were different and you never once tried throwing yourself at me. You would be surprised at the emails and letters I receive on a constant basis. Look, if you don't want to go out with me again or get to know me for yourself, I understand."

Rachel felt even worse after listening to his I-am-a-realist speech. It was obvious Rachel was a challenge for him and had he never approached her, she would've never pursued him either. She often heard stories about women dating and sleeping with their pastor, but she was never that girl. Was she becoming that girl? Would she become like the women she often heard about? Rachel was different. She had her own and was not impressed with Chris' position or material things. That's why he liked her and knew he could trust her.

"Chris, I'm sorry. I wasn't trying to hurt you; I just needed to know before we went any further."

"Don't be sorry. Trust me; it was bound to come up eventually. I'm learning how shallow these Toledo women really are; you are so different Rach. You really have your act together."

Rachel wanted to change the subject. "Well you asked when our next date would be. What do you have in mind?"

"I'm going to leave that up to you. How about you decide and it will be my treat."

Chris is the definition of a gentleman. No man—well Curtis had never made her feel like a lady the way Chris did. Even though she had her own money, the idea of man giving her the option of not spending it while in his presence was somewhat sexy to her.

The next day she booked them a king and queen spa package in Detroit for the following weekend. Curtis never did romantic stuff with Rachel while they were married, but when he was cheating on her, the credit card statements made it evident that he went all out with others.

Rachel sat in her office and reviewed her client portfolios. She looked around, thanking God for all of his blessings. She was a successful woman. Even though she was still under spiritual reconstruction, she knew her mom was right about acknowledging where her help came from.

Leaning back in her leather chair, she allowed her eyes to take a break from the computer. Her personal assistant poked her head in her office and announced she had a call from Karly Davis. Rachel looked at the phone with perplexity scribbled across her forehead. Karly and she never talked on the phone; never had a reason to. *What could she possibly want?* She thanked her assistant and answered the call on speakerphone. "Karly, what's going on Ms. Lady?'

"Hey Rach, I hope you don't mind that I got your number from your cousin. I was talking to Chris—well you know him as Pastor, but anyways he's like a big brother to me." Rachel heart started to pound at a quick tempo. She didn't want anyone to know her business. *Oh my, Karly and Melissa sometimes hangout, outside of church and if anyone was going to break the news to Melissa, it should be me and not Karly. How does Karly know about Chris and me or am I overreacting?*

Karly's voice overrode Rachel's thoughts as she continued to explain the reason for her unexpected call. "Well anyway, he told me about some of the rumors you heard. Don't listen to them; he is a good man and a great pastor. Please don't stop coming, he thinks you're such a sweet lady. Most of the people who make up stuff are just mad because they like him and he doesn't want to be with them. They are some messy, messy people. He was really hurt behind those rumors."

Rachel was flabbergasted at the fact he actually called Karly to talk about their conversation. *He must really like me, because he completely went out of his way to involve Karly.* Rachel didn't hold a long conversation because she wasn't sure if he told her about them and she didn't want to give Karly the opportunity to ask any more questions.

Rachel felt special. Suddenly she became more attracted to him. Not only was he fine, he had a sensitive side and it was obvious he cared about what Rachel thought of him. Rachel couldn't wait for their next date. Now that she addressed the rumors, she could open up to him even more.

Chapter Five

He's An Ordinary Guy

Rachel had no problem dressing for their second date. Ohio and Michigan's weather could be fickle and would go from hot to cold rather quickly. She wore tall brown knee boots over skinny jeans, a long sleeve brown tee and a cream colored vest. Her teenage cousin stayed the weekend so she didn't have to hire a sitter for the kids. Chris suggested that they meet at Starbucks, since it was centrally located between both of their residences. He didn't want Rachel to meet at his home because his housekeeper was there; Rachel didn't question it. She agreed and they met. He pulled next to her in his money green CTS. Ironically their attire was unintentionally coordinated. Rachel climbed over to the passenger side of her vehicle, suggesting Chris should drive. She loved to be chauffeured. They drove down the highway with no music. Rachel wasn't sure if he only listened to gospel and wanted to be careful not to offend him.

"What type of music do you listen to Chris?"

"What do you have sweetie?" Chris smiled at her with his perfectly shaped lips.

"I don't have any gospel in here, but I do have Mary J. Blige's new CD." She looked at him, biting down on her bottom lip.

"Oh I like Mary. I didn't know she put a new CD out. You know, you can do what you're thinking. You don't have to look at me like that, just kiss me."

I don't want to kiss you. Well I do, but not now. She disregarded his comment and turned the CD up. One song in particular was suitable for their situation. It was titled "Feel like a Woman." Chris was definitely making Rachel feel like a woman. He rocked to the music, looking at Rachel as if to say, I'll-make-you-feel-like-that-baby.

Rachel was impressed with him. Although he was a pastor, he was really just an ordinary guy. After their spa treatment, he took Rachel to the mall and bought her everything that looked good on her. He was a breath of fresh air. Rachel was truly falling for him. Chris definitely knew how to treat a lady. He made her feel like a woman and she liked it.

After their shopping extravaganza, he took Rachel to a fancy restaurant, which Rachel had never been to. It felt like a dream or a movie as he took her menu, asking permission to order for her. Either he was a perfect gentlemen or he'd done this a time or two before. They talked about everything over dinner. He told Rachel about his prior marriage engagement and how the members of his congregation ran his fiancée away. "So have you told Melissa about us?"

Rachel looked him in his eyes with sincerity. "No. I haven't told a soul. I'm a private person. Whatever goes down between you and I, is nobody's business."

Chris realized she could be trusted. She could keep a secret; his secrets that he would later disclose. She too, knew she would be able to share things with him; things that she had never told anyone. Rachel excused herself from the table and went to the restroom. When she returned to the table, he'd already paid for the bill and was waiting outside for her. He had the parking attendant pull the car around and handed her a box of chocolate. "I ran across the street and got you some chocolates. I hope you like them."

Chocolate covered strawberries are my favorite. How did he know these were my favorite? Rachel felt like a character in a movie. Silently thanking God for sending her this man, she reached over and gave him a peck on the cheek. She bit the inside of her jaw to see if it would hurt. It did, therefore she knew she wasn't dreaming. "Thank you for such a wonderful day."

"Don't mention it baby. As long as you're with me, you'll never have to want for anything." He meant what he said. They listened to Mary the whole way back to Toledo.

When they arrived at Starbucks, he invited her to come back to his place for a movie. They both pulled into his garage and went inside. His place was well decorated for a bachelor; it was big enough for a wife and kids, but there wasn't going to be a first lady anytime soon. Chris was a gentleman. They sat in the family room, watching an episode of *Law and Order*. Not one time did he try to touch her or make any advances towards her. Before Rachel departed, he gave her a tour of his honeycomb hideout.

He led her down the long corridor. Without warning he kissed her. It was the most passionate kiss Rachel had ever experienced. Again she felt like a leading star in a movie. He kissed her from the kitchen to the back door. Kissing her from her lips down to her neck, he gently placed her body against the wall. Rachel couldn't take it. If a kiss could make her feel like this, the idea of making love to this man frightened her. She broke away, dashing out of the door and into the garage towards her car. "I-I-I can't do this." His touch felt so good to the point she was afraid of feeling good. He opened the garage door and she drove away in the night air. Suddenly she felt stupid and was embarrassed by the way she left. She felt like she had to tell someone, but who could she tell? Marveling over her day, she hung her things up in her closet. *Yeah he's a pastor but, he's a man first.* She sat on the edge of her bed and daydreamed.

The next morning she decided to send him a text message. Hours went by and he never responded back. She hoped she didn't make a fool of herself or turn him off. She called and texted him the remainder of the week; he didn't respond or call back.

Rachel was confused. *Does he already have someone? Is this just some sick game he plays with young vulnerable women?* Her feelings were a little hurt and she was almost beginning to believe that Chris was a bit of an asshole. She conveniently missed church the following Sunday due to CJ being ill. In a state of disbelief, she never thought Chris would behave in such a manner. Was he upset with her because he'd spent his money and thought he should be getting a little more than what she put out? *No, that can't be it. I have my own, just like he has his own.* When the next Sunday rolled around, Rachel went to church alone. Curtis Sr. had called and wanted to spend time with their kids. He finally realized the kids had nothing to do with their divorce. Although Rachel had some reservation about them being around Leah for an entire week, she agreed. During the sermon, Rachel felt uneasy looking at Chris. At the end of service, Chris greeted Rachel as if nothing happened. Rachel was still confused; an entire week with no texting or calling. She decided not to sweat the situation or him; she didn't want to appear to be desperate. Still she couldn't resist him.

Besides, she had such a good time with him and wasn't ready for whatever they shared to end. After work on Wednesday she decided to go to bible study at St. Mary's. Wanting to be closer to Chris and God, she almost wished he hadn't pursued her. She was minding her own business and he called her up out of the blue and asked her for a date.

As she sat in Bible study taking notes, she decided not to go out with Chris anymore. Chris was being a real jerk. Although they weren't in a committed relationship, he could have given her an explanation. When it was over, Rachel didn't hang around to meet or greet anyone, not even him. The kids were still with their dad so she went home alone, popped some popcorn and watched an episode of Army Wives. At about 10 that night her phone vibrated on the sofa. It was a text message. A part of her hoped it was Chris, while the other part of her wanted to remain pissed off at him.

It read: *Hey baby. It was good seeing you tonight. How are you and the kids?*

He never asked about the kids before. He was trying to win Rachel over. She texted back and told him what she was doing. He apologized for not calling, he told her he had been out of town and his phone was messed up. Rachel bought his excuse and allowed her true feelings for him to come back. He invited her over. Rachel was reluctant to go over to his house so late. She only lived four minutes from him but she didn't believe it would be appropriate. She was missing him. She gave it a little more thought and decided to go.

Rachel pinned her hair up in a cute ponytail. She took a quick bubble bath to freshen up just in case the unthinkable was to go down. She threw on some grey sweats, a tee shirt, and a pair of flip flops and shined her lips. The garage was left open for her. She parked her Mercedes, closed the garage door and entered his home through the kitchen. He met her in the family room, picked her up and squeezed her with the type of hug you give someone that you really miss.

They cuddled up on the loveseat and watched TV. He kissed her gently. Rachel accepted his advances, deciding not to run away this time. She closed her eyes, kissing him back, allowing him to caress and squeeze her behind. His touch felt so good. He was moving in the very spot of her heart that she vowed no one else would enter after her divorce. She realized the heart does what it wants and when love calls, there's no escaping it. It no longer mattered how Melissa felt about him or that he was a preacher. He had her, she was in. She wanted him just as much as he wanted her. No longer could she fight the feeling. Chris was an ordinary man, a typical guy who liked what he liked and got whatever he wanted. The more he kissed her, the more she let down her guard. He took his shirt off to show off his physique. He had a six pack and pecs out of this world. His body was tattooed like the late rapper Tupac and he had a nipple ring. *Chris Jackson, who in the hell are you?* Rachel started sucking on his nipple ring and it drove him crazy. Who would have ever thought, that the same man who sung "God Is" every Sunday, had a sexy gangster side. Rachel was a good girl who always managed to attract bad boys. She was really hooked on him. From that point on she knew they shared a bond, she just didn't know what it was exactly.

He kissed around her belly button exposing her tattoo she got when she was in high school. "Damn Rachel, you're sexy." They kissed, laughed, and talked until the sun came up. The two had a special chemistry, one that no else could understand. How could she tell anyone, she'd fallen for a ghetto pastor that had more tattoos than her dope selling ex-husband? She couldn't, and knew that she wasn't going to. "I want to tell you all my secrets." His eyes were asking her if she could be trusted. She nodded her head and kept kissing him. "Let's go upstairs." He whispered in her ear, leading her to his bedroom.

Chapter Six

Premeditated

He already knew what he wanted before Rachel arrived. It was evident that he knew he would get it. He led her through the French doors of his bedroom. Warm vanilla scented candles were burning and Mary J. Blige was playing in the background. Rachel was nervous about what she already discerned. She wanted it, but how could she fornicate with the person who tells people not to commit that very sin. *Actually, I have never heard him preach about this and now I know why. Everyone has needs.* She wanted to ask him about his thoughts on fornication. Not wanting to ruin the mood, she just kept kissing him instead.

He gently placed her body down on his high platform bed. The white sheets smelled fresh and not a stain was present. He continued kissing her while he slipped off her clothes. His foreplay was like no other; well at least he had Curtis beat by a long stretch. He was gentle and smooth about everything he did to her. Sliding in between her legs, he wrapped her legs around his waist and began to penetrate her. Rachel made a mental note of him not wearing a condom. She was horny so it really didn't matter. She wasn't on any type of birth control. She had been with her husband for so long and never prepared herself for sex after him. Chris was working her body like he was Billy Blanks and she was on his workout plan. He was hitting spots she never knew existed. "Take it mami, take it." He kept repeating it every time she moaned. The song *Slow* by Jamie Foxx, bolted from his iPod; he sang the lyrics as he continued to grind to the beat. " . . . and I'm gone go slow-slow. Those other guys don't get it, like I get it."

*He's definit*ely *right; Curtis has never made me feel this good.* Rachel was enjoying their love making session. She was a petite little beast, taking everything he was giving her. He rolled her over placing her hands on the footboard. She held on tight while he worked her from behind. He was ten years older than she was, but he had stamina. Rachel was sweating from head to toe. It was so beautiful. They came together. He rolled her over on her side and held her tightly in his arms.

"Damn. Now that was good." She had to give him his props, still not believing what had transpired. Grabbing a warm towel, he washed her body and placed her underneath the sheets. Their naked bodies pressed up against each other and they drifted to sleep. She dreamed about doing it all over again in her sleep.

Rachel was awakened by the aroma of coffee. Chris had a tray with breakfast and a rose sitting on the nightstand for her. He was packing some clothes and singing. His voice was pleasant to hear first thing in the morning. "Are you going somewhere Chris?" Rachel sat up in the bed, keeping her nude body covered with the sheets.

"Yes darling, I have to go to Miami and tend to some, you know, church stuff. By the way, you were amazing last night." He grabbed three ties from the closet and neatly arranged them in his suitcase. "Take your time, you can let yourself out. I have to catch a flight in about an hour." He kissed her on her forehead, and then moved his lips down to her thighs. "Well I can spare three minutes mami, lay back." In three minutes he satisfied her better then Curtis did throughout their entire marriage.

He wiped his mouth with the corner of the sheet and dashed out of the room. Rachel sipped her coffee and looked around the room. She phoned her assistant to let her know she would be in by nine. There couldn't be another woman in his life. He did leave her alone in his home. It was only six in the morning so she decided to lay back down and snooze for another thirty minutes. When she woke up she showered in his master bathroom and found one of his tee-shirts to slip on until she got home. When she pulled out of his garage she noticed a burgundy colored jeep riding pass his house. It was a lady from the choir at St. Mary's. She was spying on the Pastor. Rachel skirted off leaving tire tracks in the driveway. She thought about phoning him to let him know, but she didn't want to startle him. Chris was already extra cautious and super paranoid and she didn't want to make his paranoia worse.

After she changed her clothes and got to work, she hit instant replay in her mind, thinking about the way Pastor Jackson put it down. She knew she would eventually love again. She just wasn't ready to love so soon. She went to the gym on her lunch break, feeling energized and wanting to keep her body tight for her new man.

Later on that night, she texted him to let him know she was thinking of him. He didn't respond. Not responding was becoming routine for him. Days went by and she didn't hear his voice until she showed up for Church on Sunday to hear him preach. Rachel noticed an unfamiliar face sitting next to his housekeeper. The lady stood up and introduced herself. She was from Miami. Rachel couldn't help but to stare at her; she was pissed. Chris glanced at Rachel while he was preaching and knew by the expression on her face, she was hurt. Rachel felt so used and dirty.

It was hard for her to focus on the sermon. The only thing she could see was his tattooed body and wonder if he was screwing this Miami woman too. She left church before he dismissed everyone. She couldn't take it and didn't want to attract attention from the members.

At home she waited on Curtis to bring their children home. She almost wished she could be back with her ex-husband. She figured if she was just going from one bad situation to another, she might as well had stuck it out with Curtis, at least she already knew he was up to no good. Her phone was vibrating. *Oh so now Mr. preacher-man wants to text.*

She snatched her blackberry off the coffee table. The message read: *Is everything okay? I noticed you left service before it ended.*

Seriously? She couldn't believe him. Her blood was boiling like stew on a cold winter day. She texted back without holding back her feelings: *Yeah, I seen your little girlfriend from Miami and you haven't talked to me all week, so why now?*

Her phone rang. "Hello?" She was happy to see that he was finally calling, but didn't want to let him know.

"Rachel, baby . . . It's not like that. She is one of my old members and she was in Ohio visiting her sister. Does she like me? Yes. Did I do anything with her? No. Please believe me baby."

Rachel wanted to believe that he was telling the truth, so she did. She believed every word he said.

"Can you come over? I've missed you so much?" He was so persuading without even trying.

She figured she could swing by for a little while, the kids wouldn't arrive home for another few hours and she did miss him. She agreed and pulled into his garage seven minutes later. He met her in the kitchen and handed her a box of chocolates and a bag from Bebe. Inside was a beautiful sexy black dress.

"I figured we should go somewhere on Thursday and I want you to wear that for daddy." He could be so sweet when he wasn't confusing the crap out of Rachel. Rachel hugged him and the negative feelings that she had quickly vanished. Kissing her, he lowered her to the ground by gently pulling her hair. He pulled out his penis that was pierced and shoved it into her mouth. Rachel didn't want to do it, but she wanted to keep him happy. She closed her eyes, imagining he wasn't who he was and that she wasn't doing what she was doing to him. From the sounds he was making he was enjoying it. On the marble floor of the kitchen, he made love to her. She made another mental note that he wasn't wearing a condom; still, once again her body felt so good, she dare not stop him.

When it was over she pulled down her skirt and left. She cried the whole way home. She couldn't believe she was having sex with the pastor. When she got into her house, she ran to her bedroom and stripped down naked. She scrubbed her body in the shower until her skin began to peel. She opened her mouth, allowing the shower water to rinse away any particles he had left behind.

When her kids arrived home it was hard to look at them. She felt so disgusting. How could she teach them right from wrong, if she was on the right side of wrong? She put them to bed without spending time with them.

On Wednesday she made it to Bible study early, with every intention of telling Chris how she was feeling. She didn't bother texting him all week, figuring he probably wouldn't respond anyhow. When she went to knock on his door she noticed one of the elders was in his office with him, so she quickly ran away. "Come in Sister Jones!" He motioned for the elder to leave. She walked in and nearly tripped. He chuckled and asked, "Are you okay? Shut the door and have a seat. Tell me what's on your mind."

She cleared her throat as she shut the door. "Well Chris—I feel uncomfortable being here, since we've been—you know. It's hard for me to listen and I can't take communion and . . . ."

He got up and locked the other door leading into his office. "Rachel, you're tripping. I'm going to need you to relax and get a grip." He kept a low tone. Then he did the unthinkable in the house of the Lord. He lifted her skirt, pulled down her panties, placed one hand over her mouth, and stuck his head between her legs. Rachel wanted to bite his hand. She wondered how often he did these kinds of things at church. Tears began to roll down her cheeks. She decided to close her eyes and relax until he finished. When he was done, he put one finger up to his mouth and told her to be quiet. He grabbed some Kleenex from his desk and tried to clean her off. Rachel thought it was over until he unzipped his pants. "My turn, now make daddy happy mami." Pulling his penis out, he carefully placed it in her mouth. He didn't make a sound, not even when he came.

He stuffed his penis back in his pants. "Now get upstairs, I'll be up to preach in about five minutes. I hope I've answered all of your questions Ms. Jones!" He called out to Rachel as she marched out of his office. The elder had been standing outside the door the entire time. He smiled at Rachel as if he knew what took place and then he went back into Pastor Jackson's office.

Rachel sat in the back of the church. She didn't want to be near him, but she didn't want to leave either. After service was over she met and greeted a few members. "Hello Rachel!" It was Karly. Rachel groaned under her breathe and then gave Karly a fake smile. "I was wondering if we could work out together sometimes. I really need some motivation."

"Sure Karly. Just call me whenever you're ready." Rachel hugged Pastor Jackson and left. She was definitely torn. A part of her was falling in love with Christopher Jackson, while the other part was beginning to hate Pastor Jackson. *How is it possible to have two different emotions for the same person?* She wondered where they would go tomorrow. *Since I'm really feeling him, I might as well accept him for who is and see where we end up.*

The little black dress he got for her was super sexy, so it was no secret that he was going to be showing her a great time.

Chapter Seven

Not Committed

She arrived at his house at 8 P.M. sharp on Thursday night. He walked out the side door looking debonair as usual. He motioned for his little lady to move over to the passenger seat. "Hey baby. That dress is fitting you, the way I imagined it would." He kissed her on the cheek and reversed out of the driveway.

"Babe, where are we going?" She folded her arms and batted her lashes at him. She really cared for him; especially when he wasn't ignoring her calls.

"Let's just say I have two-hundred ones and we're going to spend them mami." By the grin on his face she knew he was up to something. After a forty-five minute drive, they pulled up to Club Onyx, a popular gentlemen's club in Detroit. Rachel looked at him as if to say *I-know—you-don't-think—we're going in there.*

"Wipe that look off your face. Come on lil mama, it'll be fun."

Rachel rolled her eyes and got out of the car. He paid for them to enter and they found a table next to the stage. He ordered a few drinks and after about twenty minutes, Rachel was finally unwinding. She was feeling a little buzz as she started dancing for Chris, teasing him with her sexy little body.

A petite stripper with platinum blonde hair waltzed over to the couple and offered them a dance. They agreed and followed her to a private room. The area was dimly lit and decorated with red and black décor. They sat on a red heart shaped sofa, watching the dancer work her small frame. Chris threw a bunch of ones at her, awarding her for the entertainment. It was Rachel's first time, but she handled herself well without making it obvious how uncomfortable she really was. After the second song Chris offered the dancer a hundred dollar bill to kiss Rachel. She took the money from his hand and leaned in to kiss her. Rachel quickly turned her face and hopped up from the sofa. She was furious. It was bad enough she was being turned out by a pastor, but she had to draw the line somewhere. Chris dismissed their entertainer, allowing her to keep all of her earnings. His eyes were glossy and it was obvious that he had a little too much to drink. He grabbed Rachel by her face, throwing her back onto the heart shaped couch. "Don't ever try to embarrass me!" He slapped her with the back of his hand. Rachel had enough to drink that she didn't even feel the blow to her face. Something was going on with her mentally. Instead of getting upset, in her twisted mind, she was feeling that Chris was showing how much he really cared about her. Curtis had never hit her, but his mental and emotional abuse had her scarred. She was going through the same thing once again, equating pain to love. *He must love me; why else would he be tripping like this?* "I'm sorry Chris. I'll never disrespect you like that again."

He snatched her up from the couch and they left the club. They were supposed to have a good time and Rachel felt as if she ruined the entire night. They drove back to Toledo in complete silence. Rachel stared out the window and collected her thoughts. She would never tell anyone about this. Regardless of him being a pastor, he's a man first and had his own issues to work through. She vowed to herself that she would never judge him; she wanted to understand him. His mental state was just as twisted as hers was becoming. He needed someone who wouldn't throw his title or position in his face and she knew she was the lady for this situation. She was newly divorced and initially she went to St. Mary's seeking a relationship with God; now she wasn't sure what she was searching for. Had Curtis damaged her to the point that she would accept whatever mistreatment a man presented to her as long as she wasn't alone? She was entering another unhealthy relationship, but all she cared about was making Chris happy.

He pulled into his driveway without entering the garage. Motioning for her to climb in the back seat, he joined her. *What now?* Rachel thought silently as she remembered the incident in the church office. He pulled up her dress, had his way, and then sent her home. Rachel smiled the entire way home. After that night, she didn't hear from him until they met in church on Sunday. She was becoming accustomed to not communicating with him until he wanted sex and every now and then some quality time.

It became a Wednesday and Sunday ritual to have sex after service. He would go missing in action and then a few Sundays later; some random female would show up from Florida, sitting next to his housekeeper in Church. Rachel would question him about her intuitions she was having, only to be made to feel that she was neurotic and paranoid. During her workout sessions with Karly, she would unconsciously confirm what Rachel already knew about Chris and the other women. All the women were there for Chris' pleasure. Rachel's heart had barely healed from her divorce and already she was fallen for Chris and breaking down all over again. She was running ragged because she knew they were doing wrong. Instead of pleasing God, she was more eager to please Chris and all of his sexual fantasies.

Although Pastor Jackson had enough women to feed his sexual appetite, none of them satisfied him more than Rachel. She felt the same about him. They became codependent on each other's sins. Being that Rachel never judged him, she became his crutch. No matter how bad he treated her, when he called, she came running. Still no matter how content he was, he wanted more. She focused so much of her attention on him; she neglected spending quality time with her children. Apparently love is blind because she didn't even see how much her children needed her.

One Sunday night while lying in his bed, Rachel wrapped her arms around Chris and poured her heart out to him. "Chris, you don't understand how hard this is for me."

He could be affectionate at times. He pulled Rachel closer, kissing the top of her head. Rachel felt special when he gave her forehead kisses. They had been sleeping together a little under one year, but she felt they had been together forever. She knew what they were doing was wrong, but in her mind it would all pay off in the end. Out of all his women, she would be the chosen one.

"How hard what is for you Rachel?"

"You know Chris, being the secret first lady and no one knows but me! I don't even think you know what we are doing. Do you care about me?" Rachel broke down, burying her face in his chest.

"You are crazy. I thought we were just having fun Rachel. If you can't handle that, perhaps we shouldn't do this anymore." He was calm, making it very clear that this was nothing more than enjoyment.

Rachel was heart-broken. She wasn't ready to lose him so she tried to calm herself as best as she could. "I can handle it. I was just having a moment. I'm sorry." She didn't mean what she said, but she wasn't ready to let go. Rachel knew if she played her position and held on, his feelings would change and he would eventually grow to love her. One day he would need and want her the same way she needed and wanted him.

"So when are we gonna do something exciting mami? When are you going to give me a threesome?" Rachel was sexual and with him she discovered some freaky things about herself, however a threesome never crossed her mind. Christopher Jackson had such a hold on her; she was willing to try almost anything.

"I'll give you whatever you want, whenever you want it." She couldn't believe herself. As long as he seemed pleased, she'd say and do anything.

"Good. I want you to find someone for us baby." Nodding her head in agreement, she knew she would put it off for as long as she could. He reassured her that none of the Florida women she'd seen in church were for him, and asked her not to believe everything she had heard.

Rachel wasn't as naïve as she pretended be; she just wanted to believe that one day, the two of them could become more than secret lovers. All the while she never questioned his love for the Lord or his position. She never persecuted him and that's what he respected most about her. Although he made it plain that they weren't committed, he'd flip out if he thought Rachel was giving herself to someone other than him. Her punishment would be to endure rough painful sex. Would she really be able to handle everything he threw at her? How long would she go on being his secret enjoyment?

Chapter Eight

Threesome Love Affair

Weeks went by and Chris continued to pressure Rachel for what he had requested. Rachel wasn't trying to find anyone and would lead Chris on for as long as she could, in hopes that he would just give up. He was persistent. *There is nothing another woman can do for me; just thinking about it feels unnatural.* She thought about what her mother had initially said about her dating a pastor and she was beginning to think her mother was right. But what could she do? She wasn't ready to be alone all over again. Commitment or not, just having a piece of somebody felt good. *Some is better than none.* Besides, it didn't matter what he did when she wasn't around, when they were together it was all about her.

Never once had she questioned if heaven or God for that matter really existed, not until she started creeping with a pastor that is. If he wasn't afraid of this place called hell, then perhaps it didn't really exist. At least if she taught her children what she believed to be right, they'd stand a better chance of spending their eternal life in heaven. What she didn't realize was, by not telling Pastor Jackson he was supposed to be a better man as a member of the clergy, she was actually doing him a disservice. Even if she did gain his heart in the end, what would she really be gaining; perhaps nothing more than eternal damnation.

It got to the point where church wasn't a place to serve the Lord. Rachel was going to peep out who he would be or already had been screwing. It's amazing how much power a person can have over another person's state of mind. The same mouth that he used to taste Rachel's body with was the same mouth he used to preach the gospel with. She felt convicted; however she wasn't willing to change. She was both lost and turned out; and the sick twisted part about all of it, is that she liked it. In her mind she was his unofficial secret first lady. As long as she knew and continued to convince herself of that, it didn't matter what Chris said. If they were in a courtroom both parties would be equally guilty of tempting and tainting the other.

After a while she felt numb; she was in this situation just because she could. Chris had a lot of women, unlike Curtis; all of Chris' women were successful executive type divas. Rachel respected that about him. She learned to be exactly what he was looking for; a hush chick that allowed him to have his way and kept quiet about it. Some days he treated Rachel like horse manure and other days he treated her like the queen that she was. She took the good with bad figuring he was still more of a man then Curtis would ever be. Chris came from a long line of preachers and he was just burnt out on biblical teachings. He had even tapped danced with Buddha and Allah on a few occasions. Preaching allowed him to wear the finest clothes, drive luxury cars, and sleep with the most beautiful women. Who wouldn't play church and enjoy a semi-celebrity status?

No matter how hard Rachel worked to please him, her best would never be good enough. He knew that he would never commit to Rachel, still she was hopeful. Winter was approaching so she was getting more time than usual with Chris. At the same time, her children weren't getting as much quality time with their mother. Sexually, Chris Jackson and Rachel Jones had nearly done it all, but one thing was missing. Chris was still determined to get his threesome.

"Hello?" Rachel barely allowed the phone to ring once before answering when she noticed Chris was calling.

"What's up ma? Since you've been procrastinating on finding someone, I took the liberty of doing it myself. Freshen up and get your fine ass over here."

Rachel felt that same knot in her throat that had developed the night she beat on Curtis. Her heart was pounding. She knew this was an abomination and if hell was a real place, she didn't want to find out. She contemplated, but not for long. Whatever spell he had on her kept her obedient to his every command.

Dear Lord, please forgive me for whatever it is that is about to take place. I'm sorry for my recent behavior and transgressions. I'm glad that you are a merciful and forgiving God. I would be a liar if I told you this was going to be my last time, so I want tell you that. When Rachel prayed or talked to God she had real conversations with Him, as if He was sitting in her living room on the sofa next to her.

Rachel scrubbed her body in the shower, realizing how unclean she had become. Only God was aware of her sins. She slipped on some sexy red pajamas and leopard print heels. She was turning into the woman she should have been with her husband or perhaps she was in her good-girl-has-gone-bad stage. Was there any turning back? Rachel used to think about how her mom would feel if she found out about certain things; which prevented her from doing them. Now Rachel was so far gone, it really didn't matter.

She put on some lip gloss, and rehearsed the threesome in her mind. On the way over to Chris' house she rode with the music off and the windows rolled down. Chris greeted her at the door wearing sexy pajama pants and comfortable loafers. He handed her a glass of vodka and cranberry; she looked like she needed some help relaxing. She sipped as slow as she could. Finally she was feeling ashamed. If she had an ounce of dignity left, she'd run away, but Chris was as much of a crutch for her as she was for him. After she finished her first drink, she decided to drink until she lost herself completely. It was time to meet this mystery woman and perform for her man. *Is this what he meant in the beginning about having fun?* He told Rachel this was his first threesome, however his persistence and eagerness led her to believe different.

He kissed Rachel as they moved up the stairs. He never neglected to show her affection. Her heart was beating one hundred miles per hour. Once in the room, she noticed the mystery woman lying in the bed with her back turned to them. *She must be just as nervous as I am.* From what Rachel could see about their guest of honor, the woman had long jet black hair and well-toned arms. Chris loved a woman who worked out. He walked around to the other side of the bed and started kissing his other lady friend. Rachel felt a little jealous. She didn't know how to react. She climbed in the bed behind the third party member and began rubbing on her muscular arms. The mystery date rolled over, looking Rachel dead in her eyes.

Rachel's eyes widened. "Juan!" She couldn't believe it. She didn't want to believe it. She was hoping the vodka was playing tricks with her mind. *Were the rumors true about the church organist and Chris? Were they really secret lovers?* She bit the inside of her jaw as hard as she could until she tasted blood in her mouth. She knew there wasn't any escaping this dream, this was real. She was never comfortable about having a threesome, but she would've felt a lot better knowing that Chris had been with another woman. Her stomach began to bubble as she sat on the bed frozen. It was like time stopped. Juan looked at Rachel as if to say *yes Ms. Thang, I have your man!* The two men went to town on one another as if she wasn't there. Her buzz from the alcohol wore off quickly. She felt the same sickness she felt when Curtis would bring his other children around. She jumped out of the bed, dashed down the stairs and into her car. She drove half way down the Central Avenue strip before pulling over on the side of the road. She was in love with a man who loved another man. She opened her car and began puking her guts out. The only thing that ran across her mind was the unprotected sex she and Chris had on a regular basis.

She wanted to pray, but she couldn't. *Why do I have such bad luck with men?* She decided not to go back to St. Mary's and she refused to talk to Chris. After that incident, she made up her mind that church was not the place for her. Trying to put her life back in order, she focused and participated in positive non-religious activities and reconstructed her relationship with her children. She felt has if Chris bothered her in a time that she was most susceptible and wished that he would have left her be. She thought he was a great preacher and wished he had never introduced her to his alter-ego. *Why me? Out of all the women who were actually interested in him, why did he have to bother me?* If he would have never called her and asked her out, she would have never pursued him.

At least she learned a little bit about how a man should treat a woman, but Chris' other side, reminded her of Curtis. In her mind, a pastor was just like a neighborhood dope man; he was everybody's man. It was apparent to her that Pastor Jackson was fighting demons; ironically she felt compelled to be there for him. In the beginning she vowed that she would never judge him and she didn't want to leave him behind like the others did. She just needed some time before she could face him again.

One evening while Rachel was preparing dinner for her children there was an unexpected knock at the door. "Mommy, Mommy, Ms. Karly is at the door!" Christina was peeking out of the window at the surprise visitor. "Can I open the door Mommy?"

"No, I'll answer it baby." Rachel wiped her hands on her apron and opened the door. "Hello Karly, how can I help you?" Rachel stood at the door with an uninviting look. She had nothing against Karly, but she didn't want to be bothered or questioned.

Karly made her way through the door. "Hey Rachel, hi kids! I didn't catch you at a bad time, did I? We really miss you at church. Ooh it smells delicious in here, what are you cooking?"

"Where are my manners, come right in and make yourself at home." Rachel was being half sarcastic being that Karly had already made her way into the house. She figured if she didn't talk to her now, Karly would only come back so she may as well get it over with. "Christina, please go upstairs with your brother to play so that mommy can finish cooking and talk with Ms. Karly." Karly followed Rachel into the kitchen.

Rachel turned her back towards Karly as she chopped up some onions and other vegetables. At least if she got teary eyed she could blame it on the onions. She felt she needed to protect Chris; what the two of them shared together and who he really was. "Yeah I've been missing you guys too; I've just been working a lot. I got a load of new clients and . . ."

"Rachel you don't have to make excuses. Chris told me about you and him." Karly smiled at Rachel with an inquisitive expression written on her face. "You know he's like my brother and he usually doesn't keep any secrets from me."

"Chris told you what?" Rachel was confused. She and Chris had dated for nearly a year and he had her convinced that no one could ever find out about the two of them. *Is Karly lying? And if he did tell her anything, did he tell all? Did she know that Juan and Chris were really closet freaks?*

"He told me that he took you to dinner once and now you want more than what he is willing to give you. Because he can't give you what you really deserve, you refuse to come back to church. Me personally, I feel you should come back to the church. Girl, you are beautiful, he's not worth it, besides, between you and me, he's sleeping with about four other women in the church. The news reporter and the attorney who goes there are also head over heels for him. Just leave him alone. I didn't want to tell you this, but he's engaged to be married. I don't like his fiancée at all and . . . Oh my goodness, please stop crying. I'm sorry; I didn't mean to hurt your feelings."

Rachel couldn't fight back her tears. Once again she had been betrayed; first by her husband, now a pastor. She would have never approached Chris and he had the audacity to tell none of the truth, making her out to be a psychotic obsessed stalker. "Oh yeah, well did he tell you that we have sex every Wednesday and Sunday? How he takes me shopping, wines and dines me? Did he tell you about all the freaky things we do! And I bet he didn't tell you that he was—well he is a fuckin' fag!" Rachel told all for the first time. Her emotions got the best of her and she told more than she ever wanted to reveal.

By the time Rachel finished talking; Karly was bawling her eyes out. "He's a dog! He's no brother of mine and I definitely don't need him to preach to me! I'm confused; please tell me you're making this up. Perhaps it is true, this isn't the first time I've heard this story."

Rachel couldn't bring herself to tell Karly that her man, Juan, was also playing for the other team. "No, Karly. Don't say that. Chris doesn't need for you to judge him or leave him. Pray for him, he's obviously fighting some demons and he can't fight alone. Please don't tell him that I shared any of this. I'm hurt, but I don't want to see him hurt." Although wounded, Rachel didn't like controversy and a small part of her wanted to shield Chris. She hugged Karly, who promised to keep her visit and their conversation a secret. Rachel felt bad. This man was engaged to another woman after she did everything he asked her to do. She put her feelings aside and prayed for him, hoping Karly wouldn't run her big mouth. She had no problem telling her so-called brother's business, so why would she keep her promise to Rachel?

Rachel fed her children, but her appetite walked out of the door with Karly. She could probably deal with the fact that he was tapping on Juan's back door, more so than she could deal with the fact that someone else would be the first lady. Was Rachel not good enough? Rachel not only had the looks, she was intelligent, independent, and financially secure. Even with all of her great characteristics, it was becoming more transparent to her that something was missing. If she could only figure out what she was lacking; then she could become a better woman.

She wanted to call Chris, but what would say? Part of her wanted to tell him how she was falling in love with him and hoped he felt the same. Since the first time he asked her out, she had been working hard to show him how down she was for him; now she wanted to work hard to make his fiancée and Juan take a back seat. Everyone wants what they cannot have and as strange as it sounded, she definitely wanted Chris Jackson.

Chapter Nine

Morning Sickness

The days blew by like the wind; and for Rachel so did her life, as she marinated in depression. By looking at her, she seemed to be happy, but inside, she was dying from a broken heart. She longed to feel Chris' touch and when she was alone all she could do was cry. Exercising aided her in keeping her sanity and she could almost keep her mind off of him, except for when she met up with Karly at the gym.

Karly continued to spoon feed her information on whom and what Chris was doing. The more information she took in the more she exposed about their secret relationship. It felt good for Rachel to be able to confide in someone who wasn't judging her. She thought she found a true confidant in Karly; but she would soon learn otherwise. She hadn't talked to Chris in almost a month; although she wanted to, she felt it was best not to call. Finally, Karly convinced Rachel to come back to St. Mary's to show Chris he hadn't defeated her. She decided to wear one of the dresses he bought for her to remind him of how much he liked her.

When she arrived it felt as if all the members were staring at her as if they knew why she hadn't been there. Rachel's own guilty conscious was eating away at her. Chris began singing as he always did prior to his sermon. She noticed that when he would sing the verse of the song, that said "I love you, I need you to survive,' he turned his attention to an unfamiliar face in the audience. She was an attractive young lady who resembled the actress Halle Berry. Rachel couldn't help but focus on the new face and the beautiful ring she wore on her left hand. Chris knew that Rachel noticed his flavor of the week. Was this the fiancée who Karly had mentioned? Is this the reason why Karly was so adamant about Rachel coming to church today? Refusing to succumb to her emotional state, she kept her composure along with a smile on her face. She was looking good, allowing all of her confidence to rise up in her. After service was over she walked down to the altar as if she was a runway model. She gave Chris the biggest hug she had ever given him in church. He looked at Rachel and whispered, "I love that dress." Rachel smiled at him and walked off.

Karly was watching the entire time and when they made eye contact, she gave Rachel a thumbs-up as a form of congratulations in overcoming her fears. Rachel rolled her eyes. She couldn't believe she stooped to such a level to where she went to church just to prove a point. It didn't make her feel any better being that she was unofficially introduced to the future first lady, who apparently was not a secret. She decided that it would be best to put everything behind her and find a new church. She took the experience as a lesson learned; truly believing everything happens for a reason. Chris had some faults, but at least Rachel could admit for the most part he treated her like a lady and catered to her when they were together. Although their relationship was short-lived, she knew that Chris would always have a special place in her heart.

She was hurt, however, this time; she was smart enough to know when to walk away. It had been two weeks since she made her point-proving visit to St. Mary's and she was trying to just live her life without thinking about Chris. She should have changed her phone number. He called her out of the blue and he was furious. Evidently the one and only person she confided in told Chris everything. He was hurt. He needed someone to tell his secrets to and out of emotional distress, Rachel let him down. Once again, Rachel was feeling let down and had no one to trust. Why would Karly do such a thing? Rachel was different, although she could have told every little detail Karly shared with her about Chris, she didn't. She could have also told Karly how Juan was on the down-low or about the women in the church she'd known for a fact that he slept with, still she decided to hold it all inside. Getting on with her life would be the best thing and she was going to do just that. She never imagined that church folks would hurt you worse than people out on the streets. With all the stress and drama going on, she didn't realize she was two weeks late on getting her menstrual cycle.

Fornicating with the pastor was one thing, but being his baby momma would be a whole different story, one that she wasn't ready to tell. After building up enough nerve, she called Chris to break the news. Chris refused to answer any of her calls and when she texted him, he let it be known via text that he didn't want to hear anything she had to say. Knowing that Karly loved drama, she decided to call her to get the message to Chris.

"Hey girl, what's up? I haven't heard from you in a minute, how are you?" Karly could be the fakest, but she talked with such sincerity that Rachel was confused on whether or not she told Chris anything.

"Did you tell Chris anything I shared with you?" Rachel was candid and to the point.

"No girl, you're my friend, I wouldn't do that to a friend. If he tells you anything to that extent he's lying."

"Well I don't know who to believe, but he's not talking to me. Since you have the ability to get messages to him, please let him know that I am pregnant." Rachel slammed the phone down and within a matter of minutes she received a text from Chris.

She was nervous about reading it. It read: *Pregnant? How dare you! Things aren't going your way; therefore you want to start rumors! Rachel, I suggest you get over it!* The words ran across the screen of her phone, jabbing her in the heart every time she read them.

Rachel, being a Gemini allowed her alter ego to take over. She didn't waste her time texting; she called Chris and gave him a piece of her mind. Not even allowing him to say hello, she began to go off as soon as she heard the other end pick up. "Who the hell do you think you are Mr. Pimp, player, pastor? In case you didn't know, you're not all of that. You're not a star or a celebrity and I'm no groupie trying to come up! I don't want this anymore than you, so do us both a favor and get over yourself!" Part of Rachel felt like she was wrong for disrespecting a pastor, but the other part viewed him as typical brother in a situation such as this; so her guilt quickly vanished. Rachel was not trying to have an ex-husband and a baby's daddy.

He must have realized Rachel meant business because his whole attitude transformed. "Okay, get a test and come over, please."

Rachel was embarrassed to go to the store and buy a test. What if she ran into one of her clients or Curtis' friends? She was more concerned about what other people thought more so than she was with the test results. She pulled her Mercedes into the pharmacy parking lot, checking out the scenery before getting out of her car. She thought about how she'd pulled her car over on the side of the road to vomit after seeing Juan and Chris in the bed getting busy, realizing it was probably morning sickness all along. She allowed her long hair to wrap around her face like Cousin It. Partially disguised she walked into the store in a hasty manner. She was in and out within minutes. Why was this happening to her? Why did he choose her and then dispose of her like she was trash? These were the questions she frequently asked herself. She entered through the side door he left opened for her. He stood in the kitchen with his head down, not looking at or saying a word to Rachel. Rachel decided it was best not to say anything to upset him. She went into the bathroom, leaving the door ajar in case he wanted to witness her take the test. Perhaps this situation was payback for all the women he turned on and turned out; only to leave every last one of them hurt, confused and wondering. He could deny all the Florida women, women in the church he'd slept with, but DNA can't be denied. Finally he'd have to face the truth and be held accountable for his actions.

She completed the test, pulled her dress down, washed her hands and waited for the outcome. She felt like she was a sixteen year old girl in high school whose parents were going to be so disappointed. From day one Chris didn't wear a condom; however it was just as much her responsibility to reinforce safe sex practice. Not only could she be carrying the pastor's child, she could be carrying AIDS or some other sexually transmitted disease.

"Are you finished?" Rachel jumped at the sound of his voice. He made his way into the bathroom and grabbed the test stick from the back of the toilet. "Well it's positive. This is just great! I thought you were on birth control." He slammed his fist into the wall leaving an indentation in the wall and stormed out.

Okay that was real mature of him. He should have been more responsible. Typical. So typical. Chris was like any other man who felt he was caught up. Rachel covered her mouth with her hand in an effort to keep the sounds of her crying to a minimum. She slid out of the bathroom and headed for the side door.

"So what are you going to do Rachel? I need to know how to plan for this." He was leaving everything up to Rachel. He counseled people on issues daily, yet he couldn't offer any advice on issues that involved himself.

"Chris, you don't believe in abortion do you? You preach life, so I know you don't expect me to get rid of my baby." Rachel started crying. She was already an emotional creature, so it didn't take much for her to find some tears to shed.

"Look Rachel, just tell me what you want, so that I can address my congregation accordingly."

Rachel knew she had the upper hand and decided to use it to her advantage for the time being. "Well, you didn't address the congregation when you were screwing my brains out! You know what Chris, I need time to think. I'll talk to you some other time." She walked out the door with a huge grin on her face, feeling a bit devious. Knowing that he'd be sweating until she made a decision, had her feeling like a real boss. Rachel Michelle Jones was in charge and she loved every moment of it.

Not only would he be forced to address his congregation—how would his beautiful bride-to-be react? Perhaps she was one of those women who stood by her man no matter what he did. Perhaps she was the same way Rachel used to be about Curtis. She would feel the same pain Rachel felt when she discovered her husband's unfaithfulness. Rachel didn't wish that pain on anyone. She went home to think about what she should do. With so many people in the world not able to have children of their own, adoption was a definite possibility. *Maybe if I keep the baby I'll be the first lady after all. Now would be a good time to call Melissa and break the news to her about our relationship. Nah, that's the least of my worries right now.* She had so many options to mull over along with other people's feelings. She decided not to think about it for the rest of the night. The children were with their dad so she could relax.

Rachel couldn't help but to wonder if something was wrong with her. With all the qualities she possessed, one would think men would be falling at her feet. Instead she married a drug dealer, divorced him after being his doormat for years, only to get knocked up by a pastor who's engaged to someone else. If she wasn't living a soap opera drama, then day time television must be in major transition. She and Chris had been through some stuff. The way he made her feel when they made love showed either his feelings were involved or he was a professional lover.

Rubbing her flat belly, she wondered if it would be a boy or a girl. She wasn't fond about losing her sexy figure, but she was also pro-life. No matter what she thought or felt about what was right, she felt obligated to protect Chris' reputation. Although she had blabbed off to Karly, she couldn't imagine how the entire congregation would handle this situation. Suddenly she became more concerned about Chris losing his livelihood, than she was about the fetus she was carrying. The more she tried not to think about the situation, the more thoughts ran through her mind. With Curtis gone she needed another man to love. Perhaps Chris would grow to love her after the baby is born. Or maybe he would break one of the Ten Commandments and truly hate her for ruining his life. Rachel accepted a lot of things from her ex-husband that brought her nothing but pain on top of pain. This time around she made a pact with herself, that it would be all about her and what she wanted.

If bringing another child in this world would bring her happiness, then she was financially prepared to do so with or without Christopher Jackson. Her thoughts were so tangled up. She was just learning how to be a mother to the two children she already had. She used to think the more gifts she bought, the more they understood how much she loved them; was she prepared to instill the same values into the pastor's baby?

The more she thought about it, the angrier she became with herself. Becoming another statistic, bringing truth to what she knew to be church myths and rumors; she felt so ashamed. Thinking about how she sat in service week after week, tainted by their dirty little deeds. Rachel did Chris wrong by allowing him to sleep with her and not letting him know what they were doing could send them both straight to hell.

How was she going to explain to her children that their new sibling was the child of the pastor? How would they feel about him, other pastors, or going to church altogether. They already had to deal with their parents' divorce, as well as being introduced to their other siblings that didn't belong to their mother. Would they feel differently about the adults in their lives who were supposed to be setting good examples? Rachel was upset with herself for not thinking about all of the possibilities before she became the pastor's secret lover. Why didn't she question the fact that they were both single, and although he was a pastor, he should be free to exclusively date whoever he pleased to? He was like a wild animal, his church was a jungle, and like other young beautiful successful women, Rachel was his prey.

He preyed upon women who didn't have an initial crush on him. Making the first move, wining and dining them, and buying them expensive gifts was his way of setting the bait. He had a way with women. His aura was addicting like crack cocaine; one whiff of him and the ladies couldn't help but to come back for more. He had his moments but his flaws were definitely outweighed by his gentleman—like qualities. He found Rachel at a pivotal point in her life, he showed her how a man should treat a woman and she was hooked.

He would make a great father. He may not want this now, but he'll come around. Rachel pictured him in the hospital cutting the baby's umbilical cord and holding his first born in his arms. She imagined how he would shop for the baby if it was boy; dressing him in his same suave style. She didn't want to force a child on him, but they really didn't try to prevent this from happening either. She decided to take her emotions and place them on paper. She would list the pros and cons in an effort to narrow down her decision. *Wait a minute. What am I thinking? This is a human life, not one of my clients.* She fell to her knees, lifted her hands and cried out to God. "Lord, I know what I was doing was wrong. You know my heart so I'm going to speak candidly to you Dear Lord. Guide me Lord. Allow Chris and me to work this out for this unborn baby's sake. Help me Lord! I have no one else to turn to." She curled up in a fetal position as she continued to talk to God. She spoke to him like they were in a relationship. She lay on the ground, waiting for some sort of a sign, but nothing happened.

What's the difference between fornicating and murder? Which sin is worst? With Chris being in his late thirties, without any children, Rachel wondered how many women he may have convinced into getting an abortion or miscarried. He was a ladies' man who enjoyed great sex and refused to use a condom. Perhaps he was afraid of going into the store to purchase condoms in fear of being spotted by one of his members. *Oh Lord, no. What if he has AIDS and had some evil plot to infect as many women as possible before he expired.* Not only was she feeling physically sick, her spirit was ill.

Chapter Ten

D-Day

Rachel stood in the kitchen, kissing Chris as he prepared dinner for them. He was missing her and once she received his invite through text messaging, she didn't hesitate in making her way over there. Chris was an excellent cook. Rachel couldn't be happier to be in his company. Maybe he was coming to terms with the whole baby thing after all. Aside from the strip club incident, Chris really was a loving man. All the children in the church loved him. He was the church daddy for those who didn't have a relationship with their biological fathers. He was so supportive when it came to his junior members' education and well-being. He was definitely father material. Although it was sudden, Rachel would marry again; Chris was the perfect candidate. She figured she was there with him, while his fiancée was living it up in Miami. God had obviously answered her prayers by giving her a sign. Chris must have had a conversation with the Lord and was ready to commit to what was right; marry Rachel and raise his baby along with her two children.

Chris stirred his secret spaghetti sauce then placed the spoon in Rachel's mouth for her approval. "Uhmm, it tastes delicious babe, just like you." Rachel was famous for making her little Freudian slips towards Chris. She could relax, and be herself or whoever Chris wanted her to be.

Chris bit his bottom lip. He smiled at the woman carrying his child. "Oh, yeah, well wait until tonight mami. Now go ahead and take your seat, I'll bring your plate to you in just a second." He gave her a pat on the bottom as she walked into the dining room.

"You're not trying to poison me are you?" Rachel was half joking, but she watched enough TV to know what really goes on. Chris didn't entertain the question. She took her place at the candlelit table. He had prepared a salad and fruit tray that vividly decorated the table. Chris usually ate out at his favorite restaurant, but when he cooked, Rachel wondered if he'd secretly graduated from culinary art school.

He placed the well prepared plate of pasta in front of Rachel, and took a seat next to her with his meal in front of him. Reaching across the table to hold her hands, he lowered his head and said grace. They looked like the Huxtables minus the children. He was so romantic. He wrapped his pasta around his fork and fed it to Rachel. They had the oddest relationship. Sometimes everything would just flow, while other times Rachel wished she hadn't met him, vowing not to ever talk to him again. They smiled at each other and shared jokes as they ate dinner and enjoyed one another's company. After dinner, Chris made them a huge bowl of ice cream to split while watching an episode of Law and Order.

Rachel was happy to be in his presence. She figured they didn't have to talk about the baby as long as he accepted her. She just took it for what it was and decided they didn't have to put a label on their relationship. "You know Rachel; I really do care about you and I want you in my life. However, you know my situation, which I really don't care to discuss, but I owe you that much." He put his head down and gave Rachel an opportunity to respond.

"When you say situation, you mean your engagement, right?" Rachel wanted to be clear on what they were discussing. He nodded his head yes. Rachel's smile quickly turned sideways. It felt like he jabbed her in the chest. She glared at him as she fought back her tears.

"Rach, babe, don't trip. It's not like that. Yes I'm engaged, but there's something about you that I don't want to lose. Call me selfish, but that's how I feel."

So why don't you just marry me since I am carrying your baby. She didn't want to come across as if she were begging, so she tried to keep a nonchalant demeanor. "It is what it is. We'll see what happens, I'm not going anywhere for now." Rachel felt since he wasn't married yet, if she continued to show him love, she would come out on top. Suddenly her stomach started to cramp as the room began to spin. She felt lightheaded and as if she needed to vomit. After that moment she didn't remember anything except waking up in a hospital bed with her mom and Tausha next to her. Chris was nowhere in sight; however he went through Rachel's phone and supplied doctors with her parent's telephone number. Apparently the doctors found Coumadin in her system. How could the same poison used to kill rats get into her system?

"Hi, I'm Doctor Craig. Can I have a word with you alone?" He was a nice looking older doctor who wore a white coat and high water pants.

Rachel looked at her mom and cousin. "It's okay Doctor, you may speak in front of my family."

The tall gray-haired man cleared his throat. "Very well then," He said as he flipped through the papers on his clipboard. "Ms. Jones, I'm sorry to inform you that you have miscarried. You'll be given a D and C in the morning; this procedure will prevent hemorrhaging and start the healing process for you. We believe the poison that we found in your bloodstream may have been the cause of the miscarriage. Any idea on how you may have ingested it?"

Did Chris do this to me? Has he done this before? She shook her head no and turned her back to the doctor and her family. She wasn't in the mood for questioning. Surprisingly, neither her mom nor Tausha said a word. Her heart ached so bad, she felt like she was going to go into cardiac arrest; at least she was in the right place, although the doctor couldn't heal her from a broken heart.

"Well again, I'm sorry for your loss. I'll come back to check on you later." The doctor exited the room.

Tausha stood up over her cousin's bed with a sad look on her face. It was like they were one person sometimes, often sharing each other's pain and symptoms. "Do you want us to let you get some rest Rach?"

"No, I'll go Tausha. You stay here with her for a little bit. I need to go and check on my grandbabies." Mrs. Belmont kissed her daughter and quickly departed.

Rachel no longer cared about protecting Chris or their secret affair, especially not after being convinced that he had something to do with her miscarriage. She told Tausha everything from their first date, to her discussions with Karly, the fiancée in Miami, up until the dinner that brought her to the emergency room. She omitted his down low life, figuring she had to save a little face. Naturally her cousin was upset and was ready to deliver a major beat down.

"Girl I can't believe out of all people, your prude ass was banging the pastor! I mean, what is that like? So you were like the church whore and he was like the pulpit pimp!" Tausha couldn't help but to laugh at herself.

Rachel was laughing too, but inside she was saddened by Chris' actions. He made her feel so special by inviting her over for dinner. Then the choice that he left up to her, he took upon himself to deliberate the verdict. Sentencing their unborn child to the death penalty without warning was eating away at Rachel. How could he make such a decision as if he were God Almighty? Again she found herself questioning how many times he had done this before.

"So do you really think the pastor poisoned you? I need to know before I go knocking on his door." Tausha put her I'm-serious facial expression on.

Rachel felt tears forming in her eyes as she looked Tausha square in her face. "Taush, I don't want to believe it, but yes I'm ninety-nine point nine percent sure that he did this to me. You don't have to go knocking on his door; if God is real He'll deal with him, just like He's dealing with me right now."

"Excuse me? What do you mean if God is real? I don't give a damn about that man's title, don't you dare allow him to make you question whether or not God really exists. Have you considered this ordeal may be a test of your faith? You have been through a lot this past year and I have faith that before it gets worse, it will get better." Although Tausha made jokes about everything, she had this serious side that forces a person into self-actualization.

Rachel didn't know what to say. Tausha was right and Rachel appreciated the reality check. She had so many years of success with her self-made business; she forgot to give the Lord his props. She wasn't a bad person; however she wasn't fully doing the Lord's will. Her mom continuously told her to acknowledge where her help came from, but Rachel was too busy being a good wife and a business woman. Since she couldn't take time out to praise Him, He forced her to bow down and reflect over her life. Without God in the mix, Rachel left an open invitation for Satan, who in a short amount of time performed a number on this diva.

Lying in the hospital bed was like a day of redemption. Rachel had the opportunity to see how she was living, as well as where she was heading. If she had died that day, was she worthy enough to enter heaven's gate? This was a question she never asked herself and the answer scared her half to death. Rachel didn't have a clue where she would spend eternity. If being a decent person guaranteed her a spot in heaven, she would be fine. Today she would have to make a decision, deciding who she would serve. Once again, she would have to forgive a man that she loved, but at the same time she could no longer fornicate with him. Pastor Jackson was not worth her soul, he too would have his day.

"You're right Taush, I know He is real and I definitely needed this wakeup call. I just can't believe I ended up in this mess."

"I can't believe you didn't tell me. Think about it as D-day, just like World War II; and the initiation of liberating Europe from the Nazi occupation."

"What?" Rachel looked at Tausha with a confused expression.

"Well never mind that analogy. What I'm trying to say is, today is the day that you can liberate yourself from Chris and anything else standing in the way of you strengthening your relationship with God."

Rachel took a deep breath. "D-day, uh?" It really didn't matter what she decided to call today, the reality was just yesterday she was pregnant with the Reverend Christopher Jackson's child and today that was no longer the case. She knew she needed a healing for her soul. What she wanted more than anything was to find someone to blame. Perhaps she could start with Melissa for trying to be a friend by inviting her to St. Mary's. Or better yet she should blame Karly for pretending to be her friend just to stab her in the back. Had it not been for Curtis' infidelity, they would have still been married and she would have never been in this situation to begin with. Blame it on the reverend that turned her out when she was most vulnerable, surely he should have known better. Rachel had to blame someone, besides herself.

While on a silent quest to find someone to fault, Chris entered the hospital room. He was holding a teddy bear and bouquet of flowers. Tausha looked him up and down. "Oh, I know this isn't who I think it is? Hello sir, I'm Rachel's crazy cousin, Tausha."

Chris nodded at Tausha without introducing himself. He looked at Rachel with a remorseful look. Rachel wasn't sure if the look he had on his face was out of guilt or compassion. Rachel asked Tausha to step out of the room for a moment.

"Sure cousin, I'll be right outside the door if you need me." She sized Chris up as she walked out the door. Chris placed the flowers on the hospital desk. He placed the bear in the bed with Rachel as he kissed her forehead. He stood over her bed and began to cry. Chris' behavior was appealing to Rachel. Although he may have been the reason why she was in the condition she was in, she was convinced that he loved her. She didn't care about him being engaged; in her mind she was number one. When it came to him, she was willing to do and accept some of strangest things. *Think of today as D-day.* A small little voice reminded her of her cousin's words.

"Did you do this to me?" Rachel found the courage to push aside her mixed feelings and confront her pastor-lover-friend.

Chris couldn't stop sobbing. He started kissing her. She kissed him back. His touch made her forget about all the pain she was in. "I'm sorry baby. I had no right; I was just so scared. Please forgive me." He gave a partial confession in his apology. He really did care for her; he just couldn't afford to lose everything he worked so hard to gain. Feeling as though Rachel fit more into his personal world he needed her to do just that, which explains why he chose to marry someone else. He planned on living two lifestyles for as long as the people in his world allowed him to do so.

This was only Rachel's second relationship and already she was tired of learning and loving somebody else. She figured that having some of Chris may be better than to not have any of Chris. She was obviously confused, one moment she wanted to be done with him then the next second she wanted to share his world. Rachel didn't understand why she wanted to forgive him, however she felt it was necessary. "How many times have you done this before me Chris?" She was dying to know how many women he had planted his seed in prior to her.

"How many times have I done what Rachel?" Chris had a puzzled look on his face. He quickly grew defensive, when asked uncomfortable questions.

"How many women have you done this to? How many women have been pregnant, miscarried or aborted before me, Chris?" Rachel felt herself tearing up.

"Damn it Rachel! No one before you! You're someone special to me, don't you realize that?" He had a way with words that instantly made

Rachel feel bad for even thinking bad about him, let alone confronting him.

"I'm sorry babe. I forgive you; let's just try to put this behind us." Rachel didn't quite know why she was apologizing, but she felt the longer she kept the peace, the longer he would remain in her life. It was a sick way of thinking; she knew it but decided to just go with the flow.

Chris nodded his head in agreement. "Are you hungry? Can I get you anything?" He had convinced himself that he did nothing wrong. In his mind she was just sick and in the hospital, and he was there to comfort her as he should be. Although Rachel forgave him, she was still leery about him and didn't want to chance him bringing her another poisonous feast.

"No thanks, I just want you to get some rest." Rachel pulled the hospital sheets around her and dug the back of her head into the pillow and closed her eyes.

Chris kissed Rachel once more. "If you need anything, just call me."

Need you to do what, finish me off? Rachel kept her thoughts to herself without saying anything else.

Chris opened the door and was greeted by Tausha, who was standing outside the entire time. "Look sir, I don't know who you are or what it is you think you're doing, frankly I don't give a damn, but if you hurt my cousin . . . ." Tausha leaned in really close to him. Even though the hospital corridor was empty, she wanted to be sure no one else heard what she had to say. "If you hurt my cousin, I'll cut your testicles off and mail them to your fiancée, Mr. Pastor Man." Tausha folded her arms and gave him the death stare. She knew Rachel would be upset with her for running off at the mouth, but she needed Chris to know someone else besides Karly knew his secrets.

Chris could be sarcastic in his own way. "Oh how cute. Who are you pretending to be Wonder Woman or Cat Woman? Now you listen here you Grace Jones want-to-be, I don't take very kindly to threats. I don't know what it is Rachel may have told you, and frankly I don't give damn, but you better know who it is you're messing with, before you go messing with them." He grabbed Tausha by the face, looking deeply into her eyes. "Now if you be a good little girl and mind your business, perhaps I'll give you a sample of what I already gave your cousin." He leaned in to kiss her in the mouth.

Tausha moved away from him. She slapped Chris as hard as she possibly could. "You are a real asshole! I don't know what it is she sees in you, but I damn sure don't want to find out. Wrong female, right day! Now you figure that one out."

Chris held the side of his face, laughing at how courageous Tausha was. He walked off as she entered Rachel's room. Her blood was boiling. Looking at how peaceful Rachel was resting, she opted not to tell her about the incident. The way Tausha figured it was if she thoroughly handled a situation, why add salt to an open wound by further hurting her cousin? She bowed her head and prayed that Rachel would get the strength to get over this Chris character.

Chapter Eleven

The Truth Shall Set You Free

After being cooped up in the hospital for nearly a week, Rachel was finally released. She hadn't seen or heard from Chris since he showed up in her infirmary room with his piss poor apology. At least there was some consistency with his disappearing acts and detached emotional behaviors. It was definitely time for her to wise-up and realize he was all about himself; he did what he had to do in order to protect his reputation and congregation. As much as Rachel wanted to understand him, she couldn't subject herself to anymore pain.

Reminiscing over the times they shared, she often caught herself in a state of disbelief. She went to church on an invite to repent and rid herself of sin; ironically she committed more sin in the church than ever before. She was afraid to go to church, whether it was at St. Mary's or another house of worship. Feeling as though it was pointless, she stopped praying, tithing, and reading her Bible.

She still continued to work on her parenting skills while she became more cordial with her ex-husband. She was completely over Curtis; however her feelings for Christopher Jackson still remained. He laid hands on her in more ways than one, making it difficult to shake his spirit. She no longer desired to be the first lady, she just wanted answers. What happened in his life that made him so angry toward the female population? If she could understand him, perhaps she could truly forgive him, not only because it was the right thing to do, but by knowing that someone wronged him in the past, she could appreciate his passion for vengeance.

God said vengeance was His, but if people can take retribution in to their own hands, why serve a God that one refuses to obey? Her thought process had become massacred from the mental anguish she endured over the past year. Instead of feeling sorry for herself, she decided to keep busy and not think about Chris. Tausha set up a few dates for her with a few decent guys, but Rachel couldn't help but to compare them to the pastor and his unique style. The way they dressed, conversed, smelled and smiled reminded her nothing of Pastor Jackson, which instantly made her lose interest. He had a hold on her without even being in her presence. She realized why fornication was so wrong; a person becomes spiritually wedded to everyone they have sex with, without having an actual ceremony. Because of their strong sexual bond, Rachel was still attached to him and they hadn't communicated in months. From brief conversations with Karly, she learned that Chris was prepping for marriage with his fiancée' without a spiritual divorce decree from Rachel.

One Saturday morning while doing a little grocery shopping at Kroger's with the children, Rachel had her first run in with Pastor Jackson and the first lady-to-be. Rachel scurried down the cereal aisle, trying to avoid contact with him, but the thing about children is they don't forget people and they are determined to be seen and heard. "Hi Pastor Jackson!" Christina exclaimed. He turned down the aisle with his arm candy, kneeled down to the small Jones' height and embraced them in his arms.

Rachel was hoping he would go away quickly without introducing his guest. She definitely didn't need this right now. It was bad enough she couldn't get him out of her head, meeting the first lady under these circumstances was a slap in the face. "Hello Rachel. How are you?" He hugged her as if everything was okay between the two of them. She couldn't help but to hug him back.

Please don't do this. Rachel tried to avoid eye contact with his fiancée as she silently pleaded with him not to introduce them. "Rachel, this is Lisa. Lisa, this is Rachel Jones and her beautiful children."

"Hello Rachel." The voice was soft and almost childlike. The woman smiled at Rachel without having a clue of who she really was.

Rachel didn't want to say the wrong thing or come off rude. Deep down inside she was pissed off all over again. *How dare he do this to me! How dare he even speak to me! He has some nerve introducing me to this bitch as if I really wanted to meet to her. Does he realize I was just carrying his baby, which he intentionally caused me to lose?* "You all take care. We should be going now." *I damn sure wasn't going to say pleased to meet you because I took no pleasure in that meeting.*

Rachel didn't want to feel the way she did towards Lisa; it wasn't her fault that she was engaged to a complete stranger. She quickly threw some junk food in the grocery cart for her children and checked out as quickly as she could. "What's wrong Momma?" Christina could always tell when something was troubling her mother.

"Nothing baby, Momma's just a little tired." Rachel winked at her daughter as she continued to place food on the conveyor belt. Rachel couldn't help but to feel a little salty about the situation that had just taken place. Once at home she prepared dinner for the children and began cleaning her house in an excessive manner. She figured if she kept busy, the less time she would have to focus on the pastor. After feeding the children she played a game of Simon Says with them and practiced handwriting with CJ. Suddenly she received a text message. She kissed CJ on the forehead as she reached for her phone. "Of course it would be you." Rachel groaned under her breath at the fact that Chris was texting her. He wanted for her to know that she was on his mind and felt he should apologize for their encounter at the store. He went on to say how sorry he was for not calling; he just couldn't face her after what he did to her. Rachel rolled her eyes, erasing the message as if she never received it. She continued working with her children until she put them to bed.

Once alone with no more tasks to complete, Chris ran through her mind like a vacuum cleaner running across worn-out carpet. She wanted to text him back, but figured it was meaningless. Lisa was there with him doing only what a person who had been with Chris could imagine. Feeling like Pastor Jackson was the demon that lived inside of her; she contemplated on having an exorcism to rid herself of him. It had been a long year and Rachel was ready to throw in the towel; instead she began to hum an old church song, "I'm Not Tired Yet." It had been a while since she prayed or even talked to God, so that night she decided to give it a try. Kneeling on the side of her bed she attempted to talk to God, but when she opened her mouth, nothing would come out. Tears streamed down her face. Finally she decided to succumb to her feelings. She sent Chris a message that read: *Hey.*

Almost immediately he responded with a request to see her. Rachel never allowed him to come over while the kids were there and he had never tried to. As odd as it seemed, she felt special knowing that he wanted to be in her presence even though Lisa was in town. The truth of the matter was, he thought of Rachel as often as she thought of him and always wanted her around. She was reluctant in letting him come over even though her children were sleeping.

What if they wake up? I guess it wouldn't hurt to allow him to stop by for a few minutes. She wondered what lie he was going to tell his fiancée, as she texted him back with her approval to his request. She quickly freshened up, smoothed out her hair and put some gloss on her lips. Knowing he would arrive in less than ten minutes she peeked in on both of her children to make sure they were sleeping soundly. She snuck down the stairs and waited for his arrival. Rachel felt like she was sneaking in her own home. She never wanted to do anything that would intentionally hurt her children or make them lose respect for her.

Chris drove into the driveway with his candy apple red Range Rover. Rachel quietly pushed the front door open. He lifted her up off the ground as he hugged her. Rachel knew that he shouldn't be there. He would turn her on, make her fall in love all over again, and then do his famous disappearing act. "Chris, why are you here? Why don't you just let me be? Every time I feel like I can get over you, you magically appear. It wasn't this hard to be delivered from my ex-husband!" Rachel needed him to know what was on her mind.

Chris grabbed her hand, leading them away from the door. "Rachel, I love you. Whether you believe me or not, it's true." Rachel's attitude quickly changed. She couldn't help but to smile as she absorbed his words. Either he really had a genuine love for her or this brother had plenty of game and a gift for gab to go along with it.

"Then why are you marrying her, if you claim you love me?" Rachel shocked herself with that question. She didn't expect for him to suddenly break off his engagement and offer her the opportunity to become the Mrs. Reverend Christopher Jackson, she wasn't even sure if she would want that now. The question was relevant in her need to understand him, other men, and why people cheat. Chris was completely thrown off by the question.

"Rachel, I didn't come over here for this." Chris wrapped his arms around her as he kissed her neck. "I missed you baby, can't you just accept that and take it for what it is?"

That was just it; Rachel was tired of just accepting whatever was given to her. It was time to stand up to Chris the same way she stood up to Curtis, minus the battering incident. She didn't want to become a woman scorned; hating all men, for what one man had done to her. As much as she wanted him there, she needed him to leave her home and go back home to the woman he chose to live the rest of his life with. "I have missed you Chris. I think we should love each other from afar. Please leave, you really shouldn't be here." *I guess I just needed to see his face and speak my mind to have real closure.*

Not taking her serious because he had gotten all too familiar with their on again off again relationship, he grabbed Rachel by her face and kissed her. She couldn't help but to think about the first time their lips introduced themselves to each other. She briefly kissed him back until reality sank in. "Chris I'm serious!" Remembering the kids were in the house sleeping, she lowered her voice. "I'm no closer to God than I was on the day I first walked into your church. Now because of you I'm lost. I'm afraid to go to church and I don't even pray anymore because you make me feel like I'm praying in vain! Do you believe in God and everything you preach about, or is this just your livelihood? I'm not trying to be rude, I just need to know." She held back her tears and looked Chris square in the face. She felt like she was his height, facing her giant for the first time.

"Do I believe in God? How dare you judge me! If you have lost your faith, it most certainly is not my fault. God loves me in spite of me and that's all you need to know." The way Chris was shaking, Rachel knew she hit a nerve. He turned to walk away. Rachel grabbed his arm with a silent plea for him to hear her out.

"Chris, I'm not judging you, that's not for me to do. I'm trying to understand you and your behavior."

"Oh, so now you're a damn psychiatrist!" Anything Rachel said, Chris was prepared to bite her head off. It was almost like he transformed into someone else. Seeing the expression on Rachel's face made him calm down a bit. He saw that she was sincere in trying to value him. "Rachel, I'm truly sorry. If I could just have a glass of water and use your restroom, we can sit down and chat."

Rachel was more confused than ever. She went into the kitchen grabbed two bottles of Fiji water and a bag of chips for them to share, while Chris went to the restroom. In the den she sat on the plush sofa and wrapped a blanket made by her mother around her shoulders. Chris took a place next to her on the sofa. He poured the cool water down his throat as if he were dehydrated. He looked at Rachel with an apologetic smirk on his face. Taking a few long deep breaths he sank deeper into the couch and gazed up at the ceiling, trying to find a starting point. "I come from a long line of ministers in my family. Both of my great-grandfathers, my grandfathers, my mother, father, brother, and uncles have all answered the call. I finally answered my calling at the age of 23." Clearing his throat, he looked at Rachel to see if she was paying attention. He had her undivided attention. Placing his head in her lap, he continued to allow her to journey his background.

"My uncle Petey, who has been a pastor for the last thirty years, took me under his wing at an early age. He's my mom's brother. I was his favorite nephew out of all the rest of my brothers. He always told me how great I was and how great I would be. When I was 9, he started having sex with me. Every weekend for eight years, I was his playmate. At first I hated it, I hated him, but at least I got everything I wanted. By the time I was seventeen, I could suck a penis better than any of the high school tramps." He paused to make sure Rachel was still with him. Tears rolled down her cheeks, hitting the side of his face. He held her hand and continued his story. "At age seventeen is when I realized I couldn't keep taking it up the ass. He wanted me to start doing his friends who were also pastors and bishops. They were willing to pay me lots of money, but it wasn't right. I blamed my mother for years, even though I never told her. She had to know, mothers know everything. Sometimes I would have blood in my underwear. How could she not see those stains, if she was the only one who did the laundry? Either she didn't give a damn or she couldn't handle the truth. Since my own mother didn't care about me being raped for all those years, I vowed that I would get even with her by not caring about any woman, including her. I know it's wrong. God says vengeance is His and since I took matters in my own hands, He's really been dealing with me over the years. I don't see my uncle suffering. He has a beautiful young wife and two beautiful kids. He has a mega church, living in a million dollar home." He shook his head in disbelief. Seeing how hard Rachel was crying, he lifted up and held her tightly.

"Promise me something Rachel." Chris grabbed her by her shoulders with a serious look on his face. Rachel shook her head in agreement. "Promise me you'll protect your kids from creeps like my uncle. Promise me you'll teach them how to tell and say no. Promise me!"

Rachel felt so sick inside. She couldn't imagine anything happening to her babies. "I-I promise Chris. I'm so sorry this happened to you."

Chris kissed her on the forehead. She buried her face in his chest and continued to cry for him the way his mother should have. "Rachel, there's more to the story. I caused you to miscarry because I can't imagine bringing a child into this world; this cold cruel world that I can't protect my baby from. I am truly sorry for what I did."

Rachel nodded her head. "Chris, I forgive you."

"Thank you Rachel. Your forgiveness means a lot to me. It takes so much to forgive. I pray to God, that one day I'll forgive my uncle, even though he has yet to apologize. About Lisa; I know you don't want to talk about it, but it's only fair that I tell you . . ."

Rachel quickly interrupted him. "Chris, you don't have to do this."

"Yes, I do. You said you wanted to understand me. I feel I can trust you so please listen." He paused to give Rachel a chance to agree to hear him out. She remained silent giving him the attention he demanded. "Lisa and I are not really engaged. I've been dating her brother for the past ten years. Our engagement is a cover up. There was too much talk and speculation about my sexual orientation, so I had to do something. He's dying of AIDS. We haven't had sex in two years; ever since he tested positive."

Rachel snatched out of Chris' hold. "Don't tell me you have AIDS!" She started crying even harder.

"Rachel-Rach, listen to me. He tested positive two years ago; I tested negative and I've continued to test negative, please believe me on that. Although he and I no longer have a sexual relationship, he needs me, so I have to be there for him. He's a very wealthy man and when he dies, I'll inherit his multi-billion dollar estate and a very hefty insurance policy. I repent every day and I hope God will exonerate me. When he passes I will find my wife and start my family. Who knows maybe

I'll actually end up marrying his sister." He laughed at the idea of him really marrying Lisa.

Rachel was totally taken back. "Chris, I've heard more than I have bargained for. At least now I understand you and I promise your secret is safe with me. Everything you do, you'll have to be accountable for it one day. I love you Chris and I'm down for you. Now you should get going." She couldn't handle learning anything else.

Before leaving her suburban residence, he firmly gripped the back of her neck. "Rachel, I trust you will keep my secret. I honestly have a genuine love for you, whether you believe it to be true or not." He released the hold he had on her and disappeared out the front door.

Rachel immediately ran upstairs to look in on her children who were peacefully sleeping. She wanted to make sure they hadn't heard anything, but most importantly, she wanted to be sure they were safe. *Promise me you'll protect your kids from people like my uncle.* Rachel replayed Chris' plea over in her head. *How did I fall in love with a gay, well, bisexual pastor who happens to be a gold digger? Is it crazy that even with knowing his darkest secret I'm still in love with him?* Rachel sighed out loud as she crawled into her bed. She didn't feel like thinking or crying over her love life. All she wanted to do was sleep; she didn't even feel like dreaming.

By the time she fell asleep the alarm was chirping. She laid in bed for a little while trying to decipher whether or not last night really took place. She ran through her daily morning routine, all the while her brain was on repeat. After dropping the children off she decided to stop by her parents. Her conversation with Chris made her appreciate family a lot more.

Chapter Twelve

A Peaceful Truce

Since Rachel was a young girl she had always been a spontaneous creature. She would come up with a sudden idea and immediately act on it. She sat in the kitchen while her mother made lunch for her father. The kids were at school and her schedule was free for the rest of the afternoon. "Mom, I'm thinking about expanding my business and relocating to the Atlanta area." She ate some sliced pickles that her mom had cut for sandwiches.

"That's great, Rach! What brought about this change? Curtis isn't stalking you, is he?" Mrs. Belmont knew her daughter and figured something had to trigger her sudden interest in relocating.

"No Mom. Curtis is actually doing a great job with the kids. I just feel like it's time for me to leave my comfort zone. I've reached my stopping point in little ole' Toledo. It's time for me to do great work elsewhere. Besides, I feel like I really need to lose myself in order to find myself; I'll definitely get lost in a big city like the ATL." Rachel wasn't sure if what she was saying even made sense, but it sounded half-way good.

Mrs. Belmont peered at her daughter over her spectacles that set on her nose. “I don’t know what all of this is about, but baby you have my blessing. Now what about my grandbabies, I’m not sure if I’m ready to let them go.” She had become attached to her grandchildren. After Rachel was born she discovered she could no longer bare children and became excited when Rachel first learned she was pregnant with Christina. She didn’t want to lose her grandchildren.

“I’m glad you brought them up. I was thinking that Christina and CJ could stay here with you and dad until I got situated and kind of learn the area. Curtis will be here to help, but I would prefer if they stayed with you.” Rachel didn’t know how her mother was going to respond.

Mrs. Belmont placed the sandwiches on the table and called for her husband to join them in the kitchen. Mr. Belmont immediately answered his wife’s command and came hobbling in. He kissed his wife and placed himself next to his daughter. “Honey, Rach has decided to expand her business and relocate to Atlanta.” Mr. Belmont turned to his daughter with a proud look in his eyes. He never said much about anything, but he was always supportive. “The children would live here with us until she got acclimated to Georgia. Is that okay with you?” Mrs. Belmont already knew her husband’s response, but wanted him to feel as though he was a part of the decision making process.

“Of course my grandchildren can stay here.” Mr. Belmont bit into his sandwich ending his portion of the discussion.

The past year took Rachel on a bumpy ride; the optimistic mortal knew things would get better before they got any worse. A wise person had told her that thoughts without actions would remain a dream. Determined to put her plan in motion, she instantly made up her mind. "Well it's settled. I'm gonna be a Georgia peach!" Trying to practice her southern accent, she put great emphasis on the word peach. "I better get going. Mom and Dad, thank you." She hugged her parents and vacated their home. It was only one thing that bothered her. *How will Christina and CJ feel? I've been gone before, they'll understand. It is only temporary; they'll be back with me in six months. I gotta do what I gotta do. If I stay in Toledo much longer, I'll be crazy for sure.*

Rachel loved her hometown, but the place she loved so much reminded her of the heartache she'd experienced and all the mistakes she'd made. Perhaps she could find a church home in Atlanta and truly grow closer to the Lord as she desired to do. At any rate, if she didn't like it there, she always had family and a beautiful home to return to, as well as her flourishing Ohio based business. She picked her children up from school and later on that evening discussed her decision with them. They appeared to be alright and even if they weren't, their separation wouldn't last long. Rachel searched on-line for good areas to live in. She decided to lease an apartment before purchasing another home. She wanted to thoroughly research the demographics.

Thirty eight days later she landed in Stockbridge, Georgia just south of Atlanta. For the first two weeks she focused on decorating her apartment and developing business plans. It took her no time to meet people. Before she knew it, she was attending major events and for the first time enjoying life to the fullest. The only thing that was missing from her life was a strong bond with God. The thought of meeting another preacher made her cringe, but she knew she had to let go and stop making excuses. One night while lying in bed Rachel heard a loud thunderous voice coming from what appeared to be the ceiling. At first she thought it was a noisy neighbor until she realized the voice was talking directly to her.

"Do you think you are here for your own satisfaction and glorification? I brought you here. I needed you alone and away from your comfort zone so that you could hear my voice! I've been talking to you, but you have refused to listen. Now that I have your attention . . ." The voice slowly faded away.

Rachel sat up in her bed and looked around. She saw or heard nothing. "God?" *Am I tripping?* "Lord is that you?" There was no answer, but Rachel knew the voice was real and that she wasn't going crazy. She began to cry out and pray. From that night on she praised the Lord in everything she did. When she told her mother about her encounter, they cried and prayed together. She found a good church home and realized her experience with Chris was a test of her faith. The Lord allowed her to go from the streets to the pulpit and he never took his hands off of her, but it wasn't until she became isolated from the world that she heard his voice. After four months, her second business was thriving in Atlanta and she decided it was time to get her children.

While packing her suitcase for a return trip home, there was a sudden knock on the door. *Who could this be?* Although she was making friends, no one knew where she lived. She stopped packing and headed to the front door. Looking out the peep hole, she couldn't make out the person standing outside. "Uh, I believe you have the wrong door." There were crazy folks everywhere and she wasn't about to let one in her home.

"Rachel, it's me!" It was a familiar voice. She looked out the peep hole once more. After staring for about thirty seconds, she finally opened the door. She and the visitor stared at one another and for a moment they were both speechless. *How did you find me?* With Google and all the other search engines, locating someone in the 21st century is not a difficult task. Rachel's business was listed in the yellow pages.

She recalled feeling as if she was being followed from her office to her apartment last week, but she also thought she was imagining things. Holding a suitcase in his hand he looked at the ground and started weeping. “Rachel, he’s gone. He died three days ago. I have all the money I ever wanted, but I’m empty, I’m heartbroken. I need you. I realized I need you in my life.”

Rachel stretched out her arms and they stood in the doorway hugging. “Everything is going to be okay Chris. I’m here for you.”